SAVE ... MA!

"Can you hear me?" the man asked.

Jennifer moved her head slightly. A plump white woman carrying a medical bag smiled at her. "You're going to be all right."

"What about Sarah?" Jennifer managed to ask.

"Don't talk," the woman commanded.

"Don't try to move," the man with the mustache added.

The sound of a police siren cut into her thoughts. From the corner of her eye, she could see a medic carrying a crowbar to the passenger's side of the wreck.

18 Pine St.

Intensive Care

Written by
Stacie Johnson

Created by
WALTER DEAN MYERS

A Seth Godin Production

BANTAM BOOKS
NEW YORK · TORONTO · LONDON · SYDNEY · AUCKLAND

RL 5, age 10 and up

INTENSIVE CARE
A Bantam Book / July 1993

Thanks to Susan Korman, Betsy Gould, Amy Berkower, Fran Lebowitz, Marva Martin, Michael Cader, Margery Mandell, José Arroyo, Julie Maner, Kate Grossman, Ellen Kenny, and Lucy Wood.

18 Pine St. is a trademark of Seth Godin Productions, Inc.

ISBN 0-553-56268-1

Published simultaneously in the United States and Canada

Bantam Books are published by Bantam Books, a division of Bantam Doubleday Dell Publishing Group, Inc. Its trademark, consisting of the words "Bantam Books" and the portrayal of a rooster, is Registered in U.S. Patent and Trademark Office and in other countries. Marca Registrada. Bantam Books, 1540 Broadway, New York, New York 10036.

PRINTED IN THE UNITED STATES OF AMERICA

OPM 0 9 8 7 6 5 4 3 2 1

For Elizabeth

18 Pine St.

There is a card shop at 8 Pine Street, and a shop that sells sewing supplies at 10 Pine that's only open in the afternoons and on Saturdays if it doesn't rain. For some reason that no one seems to know or care about, there is no 12, 14, or 16 Pine. The name of the pizzeria at 18 Pine Street was Antonio's before Mr. and Mrs. Harris took it over. Mr. Harris removed Antonio's sign and just put up a sign announcing the address. By the time he got around to thinking of a name for the place, everybody was calling it 18 Pine.

The Crew at 18 Pine St.

Sarah Gordon is the heart and soul of the group. Sarah's pretty, with a great smile and a warm, caring attitude that makes her a terrific friend. Sarah's the reason that everyone shows up at 18 Pine St.

Tasha Gordon, tall, sexy, and smart, is Sarah's cousin. Since her parents died four years ago, Tasha has moved from relative to relative. Now she's living with Sarah and her family—maybe for good.

Cindy Phillips is Sarah's best friend. Cindy is petite, with dark, radiant skin and a cute nose. She wears her black hair in braids. Cindy's been Sarah's neighbor and friend since she moved from Jamaica when she was three.

Kwame Brown's only a sophomore, but that doesn't stop him from being part of the crew. Kwame's got a flattop haircut and mischievous smile. As the smartest kid in the group, he's the one Jennifer turns to for help with her homework.

Jennifer Wilson is the poor little rich girl. Her parents are divorced, and all the charge cards and clothes in the world can't make up for it. Jennifer's tall and thin, with cocoa-colored skin and a body that's made for all those designer clothes she wears.

Billy Turner is a basketball star. His good looks, sharp clothes, and thin mustache make him a star with the women as well. He's already broken Sarah's heart—and now Tasha's got her eye on him as well.

April Winter has been to ten schools in the last ten years—and she hopes she's at Murphy to stay. Her energy, blond hair, and offbeat personality make her a standout at school.

José Melendez seems to be everyone's friend. Quiet and unassuming, José is always happy to help out with a homework assignment or project.

And there's Dave Hunter, Brian Wu, and the rest of the gang. You'll meet them all in the halls of Murphy High and after school for a pizza at 18 Pine St.

One

"Shhh! Here they come!" whispered Tasha Gordon, pointing to the front of 18 Pine St. Jennifer Wilson turned and saw April Winter and Steve Adams holding hands as they walked into the pizzeria. April's blue eyes looked especially bright as she waved to her friends, and Steve, whose tall frame was crowned by an unruly crop of red hair, had a big grin on his face.

"It's about time," Jennifer commented.

"Yeah," Sarah Gordon agreed. "I was wondering when those two would get together." For months Sarah, Tasha, and Jennifer had been saying that April and Steve made a cute couple. It wasn't because they were the only two white kids in the group; it was the way their personalities meshed. April was bubbly and outgoing, and Steve was more reserved, almost shy.

The girls watched as Steve and April paid for their sodas. "I'll say one thing about this relationship,"

1

Sarah added. "It's doing wonders for Steve's posture. He's walking tall with April around."

"You got that right," said Cindy Phillips. "Remember how he used to walk with his head forward? He looked like he was searching for loose change on the ground."

Sarah laughed. Cindy's sense of humor was one of the reasons everybody liked her so much. Sarah and Cindy were best friends—they'd known each other since they were kids, when Cindy's family had first moved to Madison from Jamaica.

Jennifer gazed out the window at the late-afternoon traffic. It was Friday, warmer than normal for November, and people seemed to be driving home in a hurry. Soon I'll be driving down that street myself, Jennifer thought happily. Seeing Steve and April together had almost made her forget the big news she'd been holding back from her friends. She took her wallet out of her purse and looked at it again: a small rectangle of blue cardboard that told the world that Jennifer Wilson had a learner's permit.

The day before she'd come home from school to find the official letter peeking out between the catalogs strewn near the mail slot. She had torn open the envelope and whooped with glee when she saw the results. Her first urge had been to run to the phone and tell her friends that same afternoon, but she'd decided to wait. She knew the minute she got off the phone with one of them, that friend would call somebody else, and soon everyone would know before Jennifer could tell them herself. The Murphy High gang didn't even know she had taken the written driver's test—Jennifer hadn't wanted to be embarrassed if she failed it. Now that the permit was in her hands, Jennifer could barely wait to show them all—especially Tasha. Jennifer and Tasha got along well enough, but sometimes Jennifer felt as if there was an unspoken rivalry between them.

Tasha's parents had been killed in a car crash a few years ago. After spending time with one family member after another, she'd moved to Madison in September to live with Sarah's family. In no time at all, Tasha had become one of the most popular juniors, as well as a top basketball player on the girls' varsity team. She'd even been a fashion designer for a famous European clothing company—even though the job only lasted a few weeks. Tasha's dazzling smile and long brown hair made a lot of heads turn. Today that hair was bundled in a bright orange ribbon and flipped over the front of her shoulder.

When April and Steve sat down at their table, Jennifer decided it was time. Proudly she laid the blue card on the table. "As of yesterday," she declared, "Jennifer Wilson is moh-bile!"

"Jennifer, that's great! Congratulations!" said Sarah. She gave her a high five.

"All right, Jennifer!" Cindy cried.

Tasha glanced at the card and tossed her hair back casually over her shoulder. "Way to go," she said.

"Thank you, Tasha," said Jennifer sweetly.

Steve grinned. "No mall within a hundred-mile radius

is safe." They all laughed.

"Shoot," said Jennifer, "they weren't safe before!"

"So, when do you get the actual driver's license?" April asked.

"Sooner than later, I'll tell you that," said Jennifer.

Tasha nudged her cousin and whispered something in her ear. Sarah giggled and whispered something back. The rest of them exchanged puzzled glances.

That's rude, Jennifer thought. Sometimes she felt jealous that the Gordon cousins were so tight. The two of them were very different, but anyone could tell that they had a special bond. At Jennifer's house, it was just her mother and herself. She didn't mind living in the nicest house on the block and having privileges such as her own credit card, but there were times when she wished she had a sister to share secrets with.

Jennifer picked up the learner's permit and rested her arm on the table. The heavy silver bracelet she had borrowed from her mother's jewelry box clanked slightly. It had the desired effect.

"Wow, what a gorgeous bracelet!" said Cindy, touching it. "Is that real turquoise in there?"

"Of course," said Jennifer indignantly. She adjusted the bracelet on her wrist and glanced at Tasha, who was busy not looking at it. Jennifer wanted to tell them how much it was worth, but she was interrupted by Kwame Brown's arrival.

"You can start the party now," said Kwame. He hooked a nearby chair with his foot and pulled it over to the table so that he could sit down with his basket of onion rings. He nodded hello, then reached for the ketchup. Kwame was as smart as his black-rimmed glasses made him appear. But Kwame was also responsible for some of Murphy High's wildest parties. When he showed up and took his place behind the CD player and sound system, a boring gathering suddenly turned into an all-out dance marathon.

Steve picked up Kwame's basket of onion rings, popped one in his mouth, and passed the basket to April, who passed it around the table. When it got back to Kwame, half of the rings were gone. "You all just help yourself," he said sarcastically. "Don't worry about me. I'm just a growing boy." He ate the rest of the onion rings two at a time, dipping them in a puddle of ketchup before they disappeared.

"You're growing, all right." Tasha pointed to his stomach.

"Hey, flat as a board and hard as a rock," said Kwame, sucking his gut in.

"Oh, please!" Cindy said. "It looks like you've got a pillow under your shirt."

Kwame laughed as hard as the rest of them. He pointed his finger at Cindy. "Watch your back, Ms. Phillips," he warned.

"Ooooh," they chorused ominously.

Jennifer glanced at her watch. "Gotta run, kids," she said, standing up and grabbing her coat. As she adjusted her pink sweater, the peacock design done in metallic blue sequins glittered. She looked at Sarah. "Are we still on for tomorrow?"

Sarah nodded. Even though the Caribbean Cruise dance was more than a month away, it was time to start shopping for the perfect dress. She hoped to find something she could move in, maybe in a pastel shade that would look good next to Dave Hunter's dark blue jacket. Dave hadn't actually asked her to the dance yet, but Sarah wasn't worried. They were a definite item and it was only a matter of time. "You want to meet at the mall?" she asked Jennifer.

"No, I'll come to your place and we'll go there together, okay?" said Jennifer.

"You want to come?" said Sarah, turning to her cousin.

"I might," Tasha responded.

Suddenly Cindy cleared her throat loudly. "Excuse me," she said with a smirk, "could you do that somewhere else?"

Kwame looked up from his onion rings, and Sarah, Tasha, and Jennifer turned their heads. When April thought no one was looking, she had reached up to kiss Steve's earlobe. Steve jerked away when Cindy spoke, but by then, everyone had seen them. He looked down at the table in embarrassment. Kwame was about to tease his friend, but he stopped short when he saw how red Steve's face looked.

"I'd better go," Steve mumbled. He grabbed his book bag and his coat from the back of his chair and headed toward the door. For a second April looked bewildered. Then she stood up and glared at Cindy. "Did you have to embarrass him like that?" she hissed.

6

She grabbed her coat and book bag.

Cindy was taken aback. "I didn't mean anything by it," she murmured. But April ignored her as she hurried for the door.

The table was quiet until Kwame shook his head and whistled softly. Jennifer took off her coat and sat down again. She glanced at Tasha, who looked almost as eager as she was to talk about what had just happened.

But before they could begin, Mr. Harris, the owner of 18 Pine St., came up to their table. "Hey, who died?" he asked, looking at their serious faces. "Why is everybody so quiet?"

Sarah smiled at him. "We were just thinking."

Mr. Harris nodded. "Good, then maybe you thinkers can help me out. I'm planning to add a new pizza to the menu, and I'm having a lot of trouble coming up with a good name."

"What kind of pizza?" said Kwame, taking a sheet of paper from his book bag and clicking a pen.

"Pepperoni, sausage, spicy hamburger, and anchovies," said Mr. Harris proudly. He looked around the table for approval.

"It sounds great," said Kwame enthusiastically.

"Ugh," said Jennifer. "Four different kinds of meat? Isn't that a little much?"

"It's a premium pizza," said Mr. Harris. "One slice is guaranteed to feed even the hungriest person."

"I'll take two slices," said Kwame.

Mr. Harris smiled. "I just need a catchy name."

"How about the Heart Stopper?" Tasha murmured. Sarah giggled.

"How about the Four Seasons? It's got a classy ring to it," said Jennifer.

"I like it, but I want the name to say 'meat,' " Mr. Harris answered.

"How about the 18 Pine St. Round-Up?" said Sarah.

Kwame added it to his list. "That's good," he said. "It reminds me of cowboys. Of course, this pizza has anchovies. They didn't have those on the open prairie."

"They didn't have pizza either," Cindy pointed out.

"You got me there." Mr. Harris chuckled. "Anyway, keep looking. I'll give a free medium pie to whoever comes up with a name." He took the empty onion ring basket with him as he left.

Jennifer wasted no time in getting back to the issue. "Did you see how mad April was?"

"Let's drop it," said Cindy uncomfortably. "I thought Steve could take a joke. I didn't think he'd get mad like that."

"The funny thing was, April was the one all over him," said Tasha. She shook her head. "I never liked P.D.A."

The girls nodded, but Kwame looked confused. "P.D.A.? That sounds like a rap group."

"Public Display of Affection," Jennifer explained. When it came to relationships, she thought, Kwame might as well be in junior high.

"Jennifer, didn't you have to get going?" Sarah asked, changing the subject.

Jennifer looked at her watch and cringed. "Yikes!" she said, jumping up from the table.

"Don't forget about tomorrow!" Sarah called. "Shop till we drop!"

"Then get up and shop some more!" Jennifer said as she left.

Cindy looked at Sarah. "Is this a private mall trip, or can anybody come?" she asked with forced enthusiasm.

The city bus didn't go down Jennifer's block; it stopped two streets away. The houses here were large, with small front yards and huge back lots. The pools had been drained and covered since September, and the lawns raked meticulously of the last autumn leaves. The Wilsons' neighbors cherished their privacy and silence. Jennifer had found that out the hard way. The memory of the party she'd thrown while her mother was out of town still made her wince. When her mother had come home, the house had looked as though the football team had played the championship game inside. Jennifer had been grounded for a long time after that. But she was free now. I have my learner's permit, she reminded herself, and soon I'll get my license. And maybe a car!

As Jennifer approached her house, she saw her mother's new Saab 900 Turbo parked in the driveway. Mrs. Wilson was carrying two bags of groceries toward the front door.

"Good timing, Jennifer," said Mrs. Wilson when she

saw her daughter. "These are the last two bags."

Mrs. Wilson was forty-five, but she could easily pass for Jennifer's older sister. She ran a very successful interior design business, and she took the same care in her appearance that she showed for her clients' homes. Today she was wearing a tailored rust-colored suit, matching pumps, an emerald blouse, and exquisite gold hoop earrings.

"Sorry, Mom," Jennifer said. "I'll put the car in the garage for you."

Mrs. Wilson hesitated a second, then tossed the keys to her. She had taken her daughter to the church parking lot a few times for driving practice and was surprised at how quickly Jennifer had learned the basics. Now she watched closely as Jennifer threw her book bag on the passenger seat and climbed in on the other side.

Jennifer remembered the woman at the Department of Motor Vehicles saying that a licensed driver had to accompany her whenever she drove, but this was only a few dozen feet. She adjusted the rearview mirror, moved the seat forward an inch, put on her seat belt, and checked the hand brake to make sure it was off. Then she readjusted the mirror, started the car, and inched it into the garage with the care of a surgeon performing a brain operation.

Inside the house Jennifer dropped the car keys in the little basket on the kitchen counter where her mother always kept them. Mrs. Wilson opened the refrigerator and put away the milk and juice. Jennifer was bursting with pride, but when her mom didn't say anything about her parking job, her feelings changed to disappointment. She quickly gestured toward the cartons of Chinese take-out.

"Going out?" she asked. "Are those for me?"

"Yes." Mrs. Wilson checked her watch. "Robert is taking me to dinner. Is that food going to be enough for you?" Jennifer nodded. "I better get started on my hair, then."

There's nothing wrong with Robert Hill, Jennifer thought as she opened the carton of rice and scooped some onto a plate. He was a little on the short side, but he looked good. He had his own company, an import firm that specialized in African foods. The only trouble was that he liked Jennifer's mother. And even worse for Jennifer, Mrs. Wilson liked him.

After her parents had divorced, it had taken some time for Jennifer and her mother to begin to reestablish the closeness of their mother-daughter relationship. Just when it seemed as if they could talk easily to one another, Mrs. Wilson met and started dating Robert Hill. Jennifer began to feel left out of her mother's life and resented Robert for taking her place.

Jennifer jabbed her fork into a piece of cashew chicken. It was one of those rare Friday nights when no one she knew was throwing a party. She picked up the newspaper and looked at the movies playing in town. There was nothing interesting that she hadn't already seen, and nothing worth seeing twice. To top it off, she didn't have a boyfriend. Jennifer sighed. She put her leather book bag on the kitchen table and took out her math homework. She worked restlessly on a few problems for several minutes, then smacked the book shut and turned on the black-and-white TV on the kitchen counter instead. A stupid game show was on.

"Bye, baby," her mother called. "Don't wait up."

Jennifer saw the lights of Robert's car shining through the living room windows. She heard the front door slam, and then a softer slam as Mrs. Wilson got into Robert's car. Jennifer cleaned up the kitchen, then headed upstairs. She picked up the phone and dialed the Gordons' number. She had forgotten to set a time for their shopping trip tomorrow. Allison, Sarah's eleven-year-old sister, picked up the phone.

"Is Sarah there?" Jennifer asked.

"*Atta dip*," said Allison.

"Atta who?"

"*Atta dip*," Allison repeated. "It means 'just a minute' in the Allipam language."

Jennifer had heard stories from Sarah about the secret language Allison and her friend Pam had made up.

Allison dropped the receiver and went to look for her sister.

"You have a strange sister," Jennifer commented when Sarah got on the phone.

"You're telling me!" said Sarah.

"Is noon okay to be at your place? I want to get an early start."

"Noon is fine," said Sarah. "Tasha wants to come, okay?"

12

"Sure." Jennifer hesitated for a second. "The more the merrier."

"See you then."

"Is there anything going on tonight?" said Jennifer before Sarah could hang up.

"Tasha is going out with some friends from basketball," said Sarah. "But Dave left this afternoon to see his grandparents, and he's going to be away all weekend, so that leaves me dateless—unless you know somebody."

"If I did, I'd take him myself," Jennifer assured her. She stretched out on her bed. "What do you think about Steve and April?"

"Uh . . ." Sarah sounded distracted. "Listen, I can't talk right now. Pam is over here, and she and Allison are in the kitchen. I'm starting to smell something funny!" With a quick good-bye, she hung up.

Jennifer looked up at the ceiling. "At least I'm not the only one home tonight," she said aloud. She got up and brought her purse to her bed. Rummaging through the bottom of it, she found a slip of paper with a phone number. Tyler McPeak had given his number to her when she'd refused to give him her own. He was a big muscle-bound guy from Murphy High who had approached Jennifer at the Westcove Mall. He was older than most Murphy High kids because he was repeating twelfth grade. The football team was happy to have him for an extra year.

Jennifer dialed his number and heard the phone ring once, twice, three times. On the fourth ring, the answering machine clicked. A funky song started up, followed by Tyler's voice.

"Hey, what's up. Can't talk right now, so leave your number. If you're cute and you have a boyfriend, leave his number. I'll set him straight and get back to you..."

The message went on, but Jennifer hung up in disgust. The call had reminded her of why she hadn't given Tyler her number in the first place. The guy was so immature. Finally she grabbed the latest catalog and headed downstairs with it. The cleaning woman had set out a bowl of fruit in the dining room, and Jennifer took an apple and a banana as she walked past. In the kitchen she opened a can of diet soda and set it on the table. Then she concentrated on the catalog as she ate. With a felt-tip pen, she went through it from front to back.

PINE

Two

The idea didn't occur to Jennifer until after breakfast on Saturday. As usual, her alarm was set for 9:30 to make sure she was up for *The Kid Dooley Show.* Jennifer would have preferred to walk on hot coals than admit to her friends that she still watched that cartoon, but she got a kick out of it. When she went to the kitchen, she found her mother at the table.

"How was the date?" Jennifer asked.

"Just fine. Did you go out last night?"

"No."

"Nothing going on?" asked Mrs. Wilson absently.

Jennifer shook her head. Lately it seemed as if her mother was always preoccupied. She was staring off into space.

"What's up, Mom?" Jennifer asked. "You look like you're thinking about something."

Mrs. Wilson smiled brightly. "I have some great news," she said. "Robert knows a man who owns a condominium complex in Chicago. He wants me to fly out today to talk to him about designing the model home. Isn't that exciting?"

"You're working today? On a Saturday?" Jennifer asked.

"I'm afraid so, baby. Are you going to be all right?"

"Sure, why wouldn't I be?" Jennifer snapped. "I'm used to being alone."

"No need for that tone, Jennifer. This whole thing came up quite suddenly. Robert didn't find out about it until yesterday afternoon." Mrs. Wilson took a sip of coffee. "This is a big break for me," she said.

Jennifer wanted to be happy for her mother, but something was getting in the way. Sometimes it was hard to be the only kid, with no one else around. Stop acting like such a baby, she told herself firmly. "Good luck, Mom," she said. "I really mean it."

"I know you do." Mrs. Wilson grabbed her daughter's arm and squeezed it as she walked by. "I'm flying out in a couple of hours and I'll be back tomorrow around midday."

She wrote down a phone number on a pad. "Cherise is a sorority sister," she said. "We were very close in college. I'll be staying there tonight. Robert will be staying with family."

The words tumbled out before Jennifer could stop them.

16

"Why don't the two of you just go to a motel?" she mumbled.

"Do you want me to answer that with my hand, Jennifer Wilson?"

Jennifer snapped her head up and looked at her mother in shock. She had never heard her mother speak that way.

Jennifer blurted out a quick apology.

"Robert and I are very good friends," Mrs. Wilson said through clenched teeth. "It may lead to more, it may not. But you will never talk to your mother about her personal life, especially sex, in that crude way. Is that clear? Never!"

Jennifer bobbed her head up and down. She went back to her cereal so that her mother wouldn't see the tears forming in her eyes. Mrs. Wilson left the room. A few minutes later she returned with a tissue balled up in her hand.

"I lost my temper," she said softly, stroking Jennifer's hair. "But I feel very strongly that intimate matters should be treated with respect. I know this trip is sudden, and you and I haven't spent a lot of time together lately. But I'll make it up to you when I get back, okay? I'll give you some driving lessons. How does that sound?"

Without meeting her mother's eyes, Jennifer nodded. Mrs. Wilson kissed the top of her daughter's head and went upstairs to pack.

The last fifteen minutes of *The Kid Dooley Show* didn't cheer Jennifer up. She turned off the TV and

17

wandered back upstairs. The shower was running in her mother's bathroom. Jennifer poked her head into the master bedroom and saw her mother's expensive leather suitcase open on the bed. She had somehow found room for a tall bottle of bath gel, a bag of hair twists, three pairs of socks, spare shoes, a business suit that was still in the dry cleaner's bag, and two heavy binders with examples of her designs in slides and color photographs.

Impulsively, Jennifer picked up a sheet of paper and wrote, "I love you," on it. Then she slipped it into one of her mother's portfolios.

After Robert came by to pick up Mrs. Wilson, Jennifer turned the TV on again and lost herself in music videos. Finally, when she heard the mail slot clatter, she became conscious of the time. The clock said 11:30.

"Oh no!" Jennifer yelled. On weekends the buses ran only twice an hour. A bus was probably at the stop right now, and she had to make two transfers to get to the Gordons' house. She was going to be very late.

Jennifer kicked off her clothes and jumped into the shower. Her hair would have to stay as it was. Sometimes she didn't mind arriving late, especially if it meant making a grand entrance. But today it would only cut into their shopping time.

At first Jennifer tried to ignore the idea that was creeping into her mind. A small voice kept saying: Who'll know? Just drive to the Gordons and you can get a bus from there. But the idea was irresistible.

Before she could talk herself out of it, she pulled on a black sweater, black pants, and black patent leather laceups, and ran down the stairs. She went straight to the basket on the kitchen counter. Her mother had taken her set of keys, but there must be a spare somewhere. Jennifer saw the note with Cherise's phone number and decided she'd better keep it with her.

The top drawer of the buffet was full of cloth napkins, souvenir coasters from Italy, a set of nut picks that were still in their package, and other odds and ends. Jennifer ran her hands through the mess until she found what she was looking for: a single key. The one that started the Saab.

"Look who's finally up!" said Sarah. It was a little past noon, which was late even for her grandmother.

Miss Essie had her bathrobe wrapped around her, and a neat row of curlers clung tightly to her scalp. She squinted at her granddaughter. "Theater habits die hard," she said in a raspy voice. "And it doesn't help when you've been out at a cast party the night before."

"Did you have a good time?" Sarah asked, walking downstairs behind her. She looked out the living room window, hoping to see Jennifer coming up the walk, but there was no sign of her.

"I met a nice man from the stage crew," said Miss Essie. "We were the two oldest folks there. We went off into a corner and talked all night."

"Did he ask you out?" said Sarah, grinning.

"Ain't you a nosy somebody!" her grandmother

chided. Sarah followed her into the kitchen. Miss Essie turned the flame on under the kettle and reached for the jar of decaffeinated coffee. "Actually, he did invite me out to dinner."

"Details!" Sarah ordered. She became so involved in Miss Essie's story, neither of them heard Jennifer knocking on the door. They were both startled when she walked into the kitchen.

Jennifer laughed at their surprised reactions. She gestured behind her. Allison and her friend Pam were standing there. "Allison let me in," she said.

"I hope you don't mind the sight of my curlers," Miss Essie said. Jennifer shook her head.

They all looked up at the ceiling when they heard Tasha turn her radio up to blare out a favorite song. Sarah ran upstairs and knocked on Tasha's closed door. "Hurry up, cuz," she said. "Jennifer's here already."

Tasha opened her bedroom door a crack, and Sarah noticed with annoyance that she was still in her underwear. "I'll be ready in two minutes," Tasha promised.

"Princess Tasha will be down shortly," Sarah announced when she returned to the kitchen.

That's typical, Jennifer thought. Tasha always keeps us waiting.

"She'll be out *atta dip*," said Allison. She was wearing Malcolm X sweatpants and a pajama top. She handed her friend Pam the last of the rock-hard brownies they had made the night before.

"What other words have you come up with?" Jennifer asked.

20

"*Boocher*," said Pam.

"That means 'great,'" said Allison.

"And *lene*—which means 'beautiful, smart, and sexy,'" Allison said. "Pam and I are *tula lene*: a million times beautiful, smart, and sexy."

"You're *tula* crazy," said Sarah.

Allison looked at Pam. "What did you expect from a couple of *botongs*?"

"*Krek*." Pam sighed.

"You said it," Allison added as they walked out.

Sarah offered Jennifer a glass of orange juice, and Miss Essie told them more about the cast party. A few minutes later Sarah's patience wore out. Motioning Jennifer to follow, she strode up the stairs.

Just as they were approaching the door, Tasha emerged from her bedroom. She had her coat on and she was carrying a large piece of posterboard. "I'm ready, see? Just give me a sec." She braced the posterboard against the wall and shoved two thumbtacks into the top corners. When she stepped aside, she gestured at the wall like a hostess on a game show. "Well, what do you think?"

Despite Jennifer's annoyance, she had to admit that the collage was very inventive. Tasha had pasted different pictures on a bright orange background. A female basketball player had been cut apart and then skillfully pasted onto the board to make her look incredibly tall. Next to it stood a caricature of Orchid, a model who had caused a lot of trouble when she arrived in Madison not long ago.

21

"It's great," Jennifer heard herself saying.

"Why, Jennifer Wilson," Tasha said in a Southern accent, "I do believe you mean that. What do you think, cuz?"

Sarah didn't say anything at first. The last thing she wanted to be reminded of was Orchid's visit and the trouble which had developed between Dave and Sarah. Sometimes Tasha didn't think about anyone but herself. "I don't think you should have put those thumbtacks on the wall like that," she said finally.

Tasha forced a laugh. "Is that all you can say about it?"

"No," said Sarah evenly. "I also don't think it should be stuck in the hallway. It's not your space."

"Well, if nobody minds, I'm going to leave it right where it is." An edge was creeping into Tasha's voice.

"Let's go," Jennifer told them. "We're going to be late."

The cousins ignored her. They looked at each other silently, and Jennifer squirmed uncomfortably from the tension. Finally, Sarah stepped up to the collage and pulled it off the wall with the thumbtacks still clinging to it. She handed it to Tasha. "I think you should put it in your room."

"I think you should put it back on that wall," said Tasha, handing it back to her cousin. When Sarah headed toward Tasha's room with it, Tasha yanked it away. "I'll put this anywhere I please!"

"This is our hallway. You have your whole room to put things in," Sarah shouted. "We were waiting down-

22

stairs for nearly an hour while you were up here fooling with this."

"There's no space in there," said Tasha, gesturing toward her bedroom. "And I didn't make you wait an hour." She placed the picture against the wall. It was then that she noticed the tacks were missing. "Give me the thumbtacks, Sarah."

"You shouldn't put holes in the wall," said Sarah.

"Thank you. Now give me my thumbtacks," said Tasha, walking toward her with her hand extended.

"This is stupid," Jennifer cried. "Let's just leave this alone and go to the mall."

"You're right," said Sarah. She grabbed Jennifer's arm and headed for the stairs. Tasha grabbed her cousin's arm and spun her around.

"What is the matter with you?" Tasha shouted.

"What's the matter with *you*!" Sarah shouted back. They heard the door to Allison's bedroom opening as she and Pam came out to watch the fight. "You think you can do whatever you want?" Sarah continued. "Other people live here, too. This isn't your own personal art gallery. I don't want to look at that stupid collage every time I go to the bathroom."

"Then close your eyes!" Tasha yelled back. "I can't believe how jealous you are."

"Jealous!" said Sarah with an incredulous laugh. "Fine. There are the thumbtacks," she said, throwing them at Tasha's feet. "We'll talk about this when Mom and Dad come home. You'll just have to take it down again."

23

"Can we go now?" Jennifer pleaded.

"You two go ahead," said Tasha. "I'm going to make collages all afternoon. Have a good time, Sarah dear."

Sarah didn't reply. She took Jennifer's arm and led her down the stairs. She slammed the door and ignored the cold drizzle that hit her face. As they were cutting across the lawn toward the bus stop, Jennifer made a quick decision. Thanks to Tasha they'd already lost a lot of time. Besides, they'd get soaking wet waiting for the bus in the rain. She'd gotten here safely—why not take the car to the mall, too? Jennifer pulled Sarah over to the car.

Sarah looked surprised. "Who drove you here?"

"Nobody, I came by myself."

"But you're not supposed to be driving alone."

"I know, but I was running late," Jennifer said quickly.

"Your mother is going to kill you," said Sarah.

"She's out of town until tomorrow. Besides, I'm a safe driver," said Jennifer, trying to sound nonchalant.

"We could get Miss Essie to drive us," Sarah said hopefully.

"You don't trust me?" Jennifer pouted. "I got here all right, didn't I?"

Sarah stared at the car as she thought about it. "I'm always such a goody-goody," she muttered to herself. Her mother, the attorney, and her father, the principal of Hamilton High, a school for students who needed extra help, had certainly instilled in her the value of proper behavior. She was sick of it! She gave Jennifer a defiant look. "Ms. Wilson," she said, "let's drive to the mall and look at some dresses. And let's get out of here right away before my parents notice."

"All right!" Jennifer responded. They climbed in the Saab and she started it up. Because of the rain, she turned on the headlights as well as the windshield wipers, and cautiously backed down the driveway. Jennifer didn't have a lot of experience driving on wet roads, and she knew she needed to be extra careful.

On the way to the mall, the drizzle turned into heavy sleet. When Jennifer stole a glance in Sarah's direction, she noticed her friend grasping the door handle.

"Relax," said Jennifer as they braked at a light. "You're making me nervous."

Sarah smiled uneasily. "You're doing great, Jennifer—I just wish the conditions were better." At that moment a driver behind them began to honk his horn in short, impatient bursts. Jennifer saw that the light had turned green. As she crept out into the intersection, the driver behind her kept honking.

"All right!" said Jennifer, scowling at the rearview mirror. She pulled the car over to the curb and the angry driver maneuvered around her. He gave Jennifer a disgusted glare as he drove by. Jennifer just ignored him. Then she pulled out onto the street again.

"So does Tasha always act that way at home?" said Jennifer. "You know, trying to get her way and all?"

"Uh, there's a detour sign up ahead," said Sarah.

"That's new," said Jennifer, trying to sound calm. Almost too late she noticed that one of the streets she had planned to take was one-way. She slowed the car down in time and put on her left-turn signal. When you ride the bus, you don't notice any of this, she told herself.

The detour sign guided the traffic to a street parallel to Dawes Highway. Sections of the highway had been torn up and road crews were working to get them repaired. Up ahead the line of traffic snaked down two blocks before turning back onto the main road. Her jaw tensed as she concentrated on keeping the car moving in the stop-and-go traffic. Thankfully, there was nobody behind her this time. We're practically in the mall parking lot, she told herself. A few more miles to go. Her hands were perspiring on the steering wheel. I'm not doing this without my mom again, she decided. It isn't worth the stress.

The white van in front of her turned onto the ramp that directed traffic to the highway. Jennifer looked up at the light and saw the green left-turn arrow prompting her to go. She turned on her left-turn signal and pulled out into the intersection, ready to follow the van onto the highway.

Sarah was looking out the passenger window when she saw the truck coming down the highway toward them. She knew the driver had a stoplight—why wasn't he even slowing down? Then she noticed that his head was down, as though he were asleep. At that moment dread flooded her body. They were about to have an accident and there was nothing she could do to stop it.

26

With the sound and force of an explosion, the truck slammed the right front fender of Jennifer's car. The Saab spun on the wet highway and knocked over a row of fluorescent orange construction cones. Jennifer thought the car would never stop spinning. Then the front end slammed into something large and yellow. The last thing both girls saw before everything went black was the windshield shattering into a million icy pieces.

PINE

Three

Jennifer heard voices. When she opened her eyes, a beam from a penlight hit her pupil. She squinted, and made out the face of a skinny blond man with a bushy mustache. Rain was pelting her face. Somehow she had been removed from her mother's car and placed on a stiff board.

"Can you hear me?" the man asked.

Jennifer moved her head slightly. A plump white woman carrying a medical bag smiled at her. "You're going to be all right."

"What about Sarah?" Jennifer managed to ask.

"Don't talk," the woman commanded.

"Don't try to move," the man with the mustache added.

The sound of a police siren cut into her thoughts. From the corner of her eye, she could see a medic carrying a crowbar to the passenger's side of the wreck.

28

The two medics who were treating her suddenly lifted the backboard between them. They walked across the wet road as carefully as they could. Jennifer could see car headlights on Dawes Highway. Cars slowed down as they approached the scene. The police had stretched a yellow tape around the area. Bright flares flickered along the roadside as an officer guided traffic around the crash site.

A short, dark-haired police officer approached one of the medics who was carrying Jennifer. "Can she talk?" he asked, pointing to her.

"No, she can't," said the medic. They placed Jennifer on a metal stretcher that was standing next to the open doors of the ambulance. The roof of the ambulance closed out the light of the sky as the man pulled the stretcher inside. They strapped the stretcher to the side of the truck and locked it in place.

Jennifer overheard the policeman ask whether he could ride in the ambulance and ask a few questions. The woman said no. The world became a dim yellow color as the back doors were closed and the siren went on.

The rumbling of the vehicle made her whole body vibrate. The female medic took her blood pressure while the man flashed the penlight in her eyes again.

"Can you tell me your name?" he asked. Jennifer told him. "Do you remember what happened?"

"Yes," said Jennifer. But when she tried to tell him, the words wouldn't come out. She could picture everything clearly in her mind—the left-turn signal, glancing left, moving out into the intersection. But when she saw Sarah's face freeze at the sight of the truck, and heard her scream above the sound of the collision, Jennifer couldn't say a word.

A tear ran down her temple and touched the tip of her ear.

"Don't force it, just try to relax," the medic said gently.

Suddenly the woman squeezed one of her toes hard. "Can you feel that?"

"Yes," Jennifer replied.

She squeezed another toe, then Jennifer's hands. Each time she asked whether Jennifer could feel the touch. Jennifer said yes each time.

"My mother is going to kill me," Jennifer whispered.

"I doubt it," said the female medic with a smile. "We've never lost an accident victim to a mother yet. We're taking you to Madison County Hospital. We'll have to notify your parents. Can you give us their phone number?"

Dad could be a big help right now, she thought. Dr. Wilson was a surgeon, but Jennifer knew he was still in England with his new wife, attending a medical conference. And Mom is on her way to Chicago, she thought ruefully.

Jennifer haltingly explained this to the man, who wrote down every word. Suddenly Jennifer remembered the Gordons. They would have to be notified about Sarah. She asked the medic why Sarah wasn't in the ambulance with her.

"The other girl in the car?" the woman said. Her eyes were warm and gentle. "She was pinned between the construction vehicle you hit and the dashboard of your car. It was a little tougher to get her out."

Jennifer's head began to pound. She imagined Sarah crammed inside the wreckage, her back wrenched at a horrible angle. Maybe she's paralyzed, Jennifer thought; maybe she'll be in a wheelchair the rest of her life. Jennifer remembered seeing a boy on television who'd been paralyzed from the neck down and had to write by clutching a pencil between his teeth. Fresh tears welled up in her eyes.

"Are you in pain?" the man asked, touching her hand.

"Is Sarah crippled?" Jennifer asked. "Please tell me."

"There's no way to know that right now," said the man. "The car was banged up pretty bad. But the frame of the car took most of the abuse, and luckily both of you were wearing your seat belts." He picked up his clipboard again. "Is there a way to contact your mom in Chicago?"

Jennifer remembered the piece of paper with Cherise's telephone number. "Where's my purse?" she asked.

The woman reached into a metal box and lifted out the purse. Jennifer asked her to look for the number.

The medic found the paper with the address. She gave it to the man, who copied down the information.

She also took out Jennifer's wallet and saw the learner's permit inside. Her eyebrows shot up, but she said nothing. Jennifer also gave the paramedics the Gordons' home number.

"Thanks," the woman said. "I don't think her parents have been notified yet."

The ambulance siren shut off suddenly. Jennifer knew they were slowing down. The truck took a few wide turns, and then she heard the beeping of the reverse gear.

The light from the doors opening made Jennifer squint. An orderly grasped the head of the stretcher when it slid out of the ambulance. From Jennifer's angle, he looked as if he were seven feet tall. His face was stern, but he winked at her when he caught her eye.

The tall orderly wheeled her into the hospital and down a corridor. In a bare room a nurse asked Jennifer what seemed like a million questions. How old was she? How much did she weigh? Had she been immunized for childhood diseases? Was she allergic to penicillin? What was her doctor's name? Did she have diabetes? Epilepsy? A family history of sickle-cell anemia? Had she ever been in an accident before? Jennifer answered each question until her patience began to wear thin and her head started to pound again.

"We're going to take some X rays, then we'll take you off the board," said the nurse. "You might want to look the other way; I'm going to take a blood sample. The X ray will be in just a few minutes."

It's been more than a few minutes, Jennifer thought as she waited for the radiologist to appear. She breathed deeply to ward off the claustrophobia the backboard gave her. She tried counting the fluorescent lights, then the dots on the ceiling tiles. The smell of bleach hung in the air.

"Don't move until we put you on the bed," a different orderly commanded. The X rays had been taken, and Jennifer had to wait while they decided where to put her. They pulled the gurney next to an empty bed in a long, brightly lit ward. Jennifer could hear a girl crying farther down the room. She winced as they moved her onto the bed. A nurse was pulling a curtain around the bed as the paramedic with the bushy mustache walked in. He had Jennifer's purse in his hand.

"I just want to let you know we reached Cherise," he said, setting the purse down. "She's buying another plane ticket so your mother can come right back."

"What about my X rays? What about Sarah?"

"Hey," the paramedic said. "I just bring 'em in." He grinned at her and then added in a whisper, "I'll give you my unprofessional opinion. If they took you off the backboard, you don't have any spinal fractures. And you didn't break any other bones. So I'd say you've got whiplash, cuts, and some nasty bruises—nothing more." He paused. "You were very lucky."

Four

"Just a case of whiplash, some abrasions and contusions, nothing more," said the doctor to a nurse. He looked down at Jennifer. "You were a very lucky girl."

When Jennifer asked about her friend, the doctor patted her head and looked at the clipboard. "Let's take care of Jennifer Wilson first. Your X rays show no broken bones, but you're going to be in some pain for the next few days. If the pain gets unbearable, we'll put you in a neck brace, but I don't think it'll be necessary." He looked at her closely. "Do you think you can answer some questions about the accident?" When Jennifer nodded, he motioned the nurse to let in the policeman.

It was the same one who had been at the accident scene. He had a leather-bound notepad flipped open to a blank page, and a pen was clipped to the side of it. He wasn't much taller than she was, Jennifer noticed. He

34

gave her a quick smile as he approached the bed.

"I'm Officer Edelman," he said. "Can you recall the accident?"

Now that Jennifer knew she wasn't badly injured, it was time to face the music. She had been driving illegally and she had crashed into some kind of construction machine. She had totaled a brand-new car and nearly killed her friend. She was in big trouble.

". . . I said, can you recall the events of this afternoon, Ms. Wilson?" The policeman interrupted her thoughts. He cocked an eyebrow when Jennifer didn't respond. "Do you want me to get the doctor?"

Jennifer shook her head. "I was just trying to remember." She took a deep breath and told him everything she could recall. The policeman looked perplexed when she described how the truck had hit them. He asked her to repeat certain parts of the story over and over. Jennifer got the impression that he was testing her to see whether she was holding something back or changing the story. Her suspicion was confirmed when he looked at her and asked bluntly, "Were you drinking alcohol or using any other intoxicants earlier this afternoon or within the past three days?"

"Of course not!" Jennifer cried. Officer Edelman's face remained impassive.

"The car is registered to a Saundra Wilson. Is she your mother?"

Jennifer nodded, and Officer Edelman made a note in his notebook. "Will I have to go to jail?" Jennifer asked meekly.

"I don't think so," replied Officer Edelman. "Let's get back to the accident. Do you remember what kind of truck hit you?"

"It was huge, that's all I know. It felt like a cement truck."

"Do you remember what color it was?"

"Blue. Or maybe dark green. I'm not really sure. All I got was a glimpse," she told him.

"Were there any markings on the grille that might tell you what kind of truck it was? Did it have a distinctive symbol, or a bulldog on the hood ornament?"

"No," Jennifer said. "I don't remember anything like that."

"Did you get a look at the driver?"

Jennifer closed her eyes. She remembered glancing to the right, seeing Sarah's expression, and looking toward the truck. Something about the face of the driver stirred her memory, but she didn't know what it was. The policeman prompted her: Was it a male or female? Black or white? Long hair? Glasses? Beard? Light-colored shirt? Young? Old?

"Sarah probably got a better look than I did. I'm pretty sure it wasn't a woman," said Jennifer. She closed her eyes and tried to concentrate, but when she squeezed her lids shut, her headache got worse. "White man," she said through clenched teeth. "Young, I think. And short hair. Didn't you find him?"

"We didn't find any evidence of another vehicle at the scene of the accident," said the officer.

Jennifer thought she had heard wrong. "What?" she said.

"The passenger's side of the car came to rest on a steamroller," said Edelman, referring to his notes. "According to my partner's report from the scene, the front fender of your car got smashed when it hit a stationary vehicle, possibly from the driver losing control on the slippery roads." He looked up at Jennifer, who was staring at him in disbelief. "I'm not saying you're lying, but that's what the accident looks like."

The policeman waited for her to say something. Jennifer remembered a TV detective program in which the hero had to track down a hit-and-run driver. "Couldn't you check my car for paint scrapes? That would tell you the color of the truck."

Officer Edelman smiled. "Not if he hit your fender, as you said. He would have smashed his grille, and busted a headlight. You see," he said, making his hands imitate the collision. "We didn't find anything like that. No skid marks—"

"He wasn't slowing down," Jennifer interrupted.

"And we didn't find any glass or pieces of the bumper. There would have been something."

"I know what I saw," Jennifer said hotly. "And you can ask Sarah if you don't believe me!"

"I will," the officer promised as he closed his notebook. "If you remember anything else, call me, okay?"

Jennifer nodded, and the officer walked out. She fought back the urge to cry when the awful truth suddenly became clear to her: *Whoever had hit her car had gotten away!*

Mr. Gordon was talking to a school board member when the call-waiting beep interrupted his conversation. He clicked the button on the receiver, ready to tell one of his daughters' friends to call back later. He sat down numbly when instead he heard an older woman's voice saying the words "hospital" and "Sarah."

Mrs. Gordon looked up from her magazine and was shocked by Mr. Gordon's stricken expression. "What is it?" she mouthed.

He held up his hand and kept listening. "I'm on my way," he said finally.

Tasha was walking past when her uncle hung up the phone. "Sarah's been in an accident," he said to his wife. A small noise escaped from Mrs. Gordon's throat and Tasha gasped. They both hurried to the hall closet and grabbed their coats.

"Maybe you should stay here," Mrs. Gordon said to her niece. "It could be very serious."

Tasha gave her a pleading look. Her eyes were already brimming with tears. "I want to be with you both," she whispered.

Mr. Gordon looked down at his niece and saw how strongly she resembled his brother. Tasha had lost both her mother and her father in a car crash, and he understood how important it was for her not to be alone. He gave his wife a meaningful look. "Let's go," he said.

Jennifer didn't know how long she had been sleeping. When she raised her wrist, she saw they had taken her watch away. The top of her left hand was crisscrossed with tiny cuts. She could feel the bruise in her left shoulder pounding as she put her hand down.

It felt as if an eternity had passed. They forgot about me, she thought. There was a skylight in the middle of the room and Jennifer could see above the curtain. The sky was still gray. She heard the curtain being pulled back and saw Sarah's mother coming toward her. Mrs. Gordon's lips were pressed together, and her eyes were red-rimmed but dry. She wore no makeup, and under her overcoat Jennifer saw faded red sweatpants and sweatshirt.

"Mrs. Gordon, I'm so sorry," Jennifer cried. It hurt to sit up, but Jennifer reached out to her and Mrs. Gordon held her close as she sobbed.

"It's okay, Jennifer. Everything will be fine," Mrs. Gordon said soothingly.

"Can Sarah talk?"

"She's still unconscious, I'm afraid."

"Mrs. Gordon, I know I shouldn't have been driving without an adult, but the accident wasn't my fault. I was hit by a truck, I swear it."

"Nobody is blaming you, Jennifer. Just try to get some rest, okay?"

"Where is Sarah now? Can I see her?" Jennifer pleaded.

"She's under observation in the Head Trauma Unit. The doctors are looking at her right now. Her vital functions are fine—there was no internal bleeding . . ." Mrs. Gordon's voice trailed away. "I should get back there," she said, straightening up. "Your mother contacted the hospital. She said the hospital could release you into my custody."

"Mrs. Gordon, is Sarah going to be paralyzed?" Jennifer asked.

Mrs. Gordon shook her head. "I'm not sure, honey. Right now they seem more concerned about brain damage."

Jennifer began to cry again.

"Get yourself together, Jennifer," said Mrs. Gordon softly. "As soon as I know anything more, I'll come upstairs and tell you."

Jennifer nodded and wiped her eyes.

A nurse came by shortly afterward with two aspirin in a tiny paper cup. Jennifer felt the pain receding as the pills took effect. Later a young intern poked his head in as he made his rounds. He was black, with a broad open face and eyes that crinkled at the corners. He had a lean tennis player's build and was dressed in a loose green cotton shirt and matching pants. Jennifer asked him what time it was.

"Three-fifteen," he said.

"That's it?" Jennifer said. "It seems like I've been here for ten hours!"

"Time flies when you're having fun," he said with a grin. Jennifer caught a glimpse of his name tag: S. Mitchell. The intern checked the clipboard at the foot of her bed. "Ahh, Jennifer Wilson. Whiplash. You kids shouldn't dance so fast," he said with a smile.

Jennifer was too distraught to smile back. "Will I have to stay here overnight?"

The intern shook his head. "Probably not," he replied as he scanned the clipboard. "You'll be out pretty soon, I guess. As for the whiplash, you'll have headaches for about a week, maybe longer. Your best bet is to rest, don't drink alcohol, and take it easy with physical activities."

She shook her head sadly. "No dancing, huh?" she said.

He looked up and shot her a perfect white smile. "Well, no *fast* dancing."

Poor Sarah, Jennifer though. She can't even walk, let alone dance.

Mrs. Gordon appeared again soon after the intern left. "Do you still want to see Sarah?" she asked. Jennifer nodded and they called a nurse, who helped her out of the bed and insisted she sit in a wheelchair. This is ridiculous, Jennifer thought as she sat down, but she didn't want to argue in front of Sarah's mother.

"Sarah still hasn't regained consciousness," Mrs. Gordon said in the elevator.

Jennifer's heart sank. The doors opened and the nurse pushed the wheelchair out into a hallway where the walls were painted blue. The first floor had been white and red, Jennifer remembered. The blue hallway didn't have as many people milling around, and Jennifer felt a mounting dread as she was pushed toward the glass doors where Head Trauma Unit was stenciled in bold letters.

Mrs. Gordon walked to a second door and pushed it open. The first things Jennifer saw were the tubes. They seemed to be snaking in and out of every spot on Sarah's body. One tube was in her nose, another in her arm; a third wriggled out from under the sheets. Two patches taped to Sarah's chest were connected to heart monitors. Jennifer let out a soft cry.

Tasha and Mr. Gordon were sitting in the two chairs. Mr. Gordon got up and walked toward Jennifer. "How are you, Jennifer?" he asked. He seemed to want to comfort her. But when Tasha came up behind her uncle, there was hate in her eyes.

"How could you be so stupid!" she hissed at Jennifer.

Jennifer began to sob. Mr. Gordon grabbed his niece by the arm. "Stop it, Tasha!" he said through clenched teeth.

"It's true, Mr. Gordon," said Jennifer, stealing a look at Sarah in the bed. Sarah's head rested on a thin pillow, and her arms seemed to have sunk into the mattress. "I did a really stupid thing."

Mr. Gordon asked Tasha to wait outside. As the door closed Jennifer could hear her crying, too.

"Jennifer, exactly what happened?" said Mrs. Gordon.

She told them the whole story from the moment she left the Gordons' home to the time she woke up on the backboard.

"You say you were hit by a truck?" said Mr. Gordon, furrowing his brow. "That's strange," he said when Jennifer nodded. "The police didn't say anything about a truck."

"It's true!" said Jennifer. She cursed Officer Edelman silently for not believing her story. "I didn't make it up. I took the car without permission, but the accident wasn't my fault."

"All right," said Mr. Gordon soothingly, but he remained perplexed.

A beep went off in one of the machines at the head of Sarah's bed and a nurse came in with a bag full of a clear plastic liquid. A slight hissing sound came from the machine as she disconnected the empty bag and attached the new one. Jennifer felt as if she was going to be sick.

Before they wheeled her back to the main floor, Jennifer took one last look at Sarah. Her stomach flip-flopped. We would be trying out dresses at the mall right now, Jennifer thought. If only I hadn't been such an idiot!

The doctor examined Jennifer one last time before releasing her to Mrs. Gordon. "Your mother won't be back until this evening," said Mrs. Gordon. "And I don't want to leave the hospital, so our neighbor is coming for you. Do you want Mrs. Brennan to drop you off at our house? You're welcome to stay with us until your mother comes home."

"No, thank you," said Jennifer. She felt tired again, and all she wanted was to sleep in her own bed.

At home she flipped a few lights on around the house and went straight to her room. She wanted to pray, but then she remembered guiltily that she only prayed when she wanted something. This time she gave thanks for surviving the accident, and pleaded that Sarah would recover soon.

The phone rang in her room. It was Tasha. "I'm sorry about what happened in the hospital," she said in a hoarse voice. "You must feel bad enough without me screaming at you. I . . . I just felt so mad."

"It's okay, Tasha. I don't blame you a bit."

"And Sarah and I had that stupid fight about the collage. She was right. I shouldn't have put it in the hall."

"It doesn't matter," said Jennifer. "I'm really sorry, Tasha. I keep thinking if only I had waited a few seconds before pulling out, that idiot would have driven by. If only—"

"If only I had gone with you," Tasha broke in. "You wouldn't have left our house when you did."

"This has nothing to do with that," said Jennifer. "I was the fool. I should have taken that stupid bus! Anything new with Sarah?"

"They don't know much yet," said Tasha in a worried tone. "As long as she's out, all they can do is feed her and monitor her body. I overheard my uncle asking the doctor if her brain was injured. She said she didn't think so, but she can't promise anything."

At Jennifer's house headlights turned into the driveway.

"My mom is here," said Jennifer. "I have to go."

44

They said good-bye, and Jennifer walked downstairs, prepared for the worst.

Mrs. Wilson rushed in and hugged her daughter as Jennifer broke into sobs. "It's all right, baby," Mrs. Wilson said over and over. "It's all right."

"Mom, I'm sorry."

"Never mind that." Her mother stepped back and looked at Jennifer's face anxiously. "Are you sure you're okay?"

Jennifer nodded. "But Sarah is still in the hospital."

"I know," said Mrs. Wilson. Jennifer looked over her mother's shoulder and saw Robert Hill standing in the doorway. His usually smiling face looked somber. Mrs. Wilson looked back, too. "Thank you, Robert, I'll call you tomorrow."

"I ruined your business trip," Jennifer murmured as the door closed.

"Don't even think about that," said Mrs. Wilson. She guided Jennifer to the white leather sofa in the living room and helped her stretch out on it.

If my daughter had totaled my car, I would have killed her by now, Jennifer thought. But her mom was being totally cool about the accident. Mrs. Wilson disappeared and came back with a glass of orange juice.

"When you're ready to talk," Mrs. Wilson said, "I want you to tell me everything that happened."

"I was driving—"

"No," Mrs. Wilson interrupted. "Start with 'Good-bye, Mom. Have a good trip!'"

Five

When Jennifer woke up on Sunday, everything still ached. Still she was glad to be awake. The nightmares about the accident had been terrible. She kept seeing Sarah's body hooked up to the clear tubes and wires. When Jennifer went downstairs, her mother insisted they make a special visit to their family doctor. He confirmed what they had told her in the hospital: whiplash.

"You'll hurt, but you'll heal," he said.

Sarah's fate wasn't so cheery. Jennifer kept calling the Gordons' for reports, but the news remained the same. She avoided calls from her other friends—she was sure that they were all mad at her and would tell her how stupid she'd been. She dreaded going to school the next day.

On Sunday evening Mrs. Wilson asked Jennifer to come downstairs. She motioned for her to sit down and

46

then talked about the importance of obeying laws and acting responsibly. At the end of her speech, she added, "You're grounded for a month."

Normally Jennifer threw a fit when she was grounded, but this time she barely protested. For as long as Sarah was unconscious, Jennifer wouldn't feel right going out.

"I've given it a lot of thought," said Mrs. Wilson. "And I think I'm being more than fair. I want you to come straight home after school. No exceptions—including Friday night."

Jennifer just nodded.

On Monday Mrs. Wilson drove Jennifer to school in a loaner car that the insurance company had given her. News of the accident had spread all over the school. All day as Jennifer walked through the halls at Murphy High, students stared at her.

She didn't meet up with any of her friends until later that morning. She was sitting on a bench near the practical arts rooms when Cindy and Kwame sat down on opposite sides of her. "How do you feel?" asked Cindy anxiously. "We tried calling you on Sunday, but your mom said you were sleeping."

"I'm okay," Jennifer said. She was glad Cindy wasn't angry at her. Sarah was Cindy's best friend, and Jennifer had wondered whether Cindy would blame her for the accident. "How's Dave doing?" she asked nervously. She certainly didn't want to face him.

Cindy shrugged. "Nobody's heard from him since the accident happened. He must be really shaken up."

47

Kwame nodded and pointed to an open page of the newspaper. "You're famous." Jennifer glanced down. The police log of burglaries, accidents, and DWI convictions was published twice a week in *The Madison Advocate*. Jennifer saw her accident report stuck between an assault and a suspicious barn fire.

"Teen Loses Control of Car" said the headline. "A 16-year-old Madison girl lost control of her car and struck a construction site at 12:45 P.M. on Saturday."

Jennifer read the rest of the report. There was no mention of any truck. She threw the paper on the floor.

"That's not what happened!" she cried. "We were hit by a truck! Sarah will back me up, I know it." She quickly told her friends exactly what had happened.

Kwame put his hand on her shoulder, calming her. "If you want," he said thoughtfully, "we could try to look for the truck. It has to be pretty banged up."

"Oh sure," said Cindy sarcastically. "We'll just split Madison down the middle and look at all the trucks."

"Besides, the driver could have just been passing through town," said Jennifer.

Kwame shrugged. "I think it's worth a try."

Jennifer looked at Kwame. Maybe the truck was still somewhere in town. Maybe someone had seen it and . . . And what? she asked herself. Suddenly it seemed hopeless again.

At lunch Jennifer joined Steve, Kwame, and Cindy. When Tasha showed up a few minutes later, she announced that Sarah was still unconscious. "I called my aunt after homeroom this morning. She's been practically living at the hospital since Saturday."

Jennifer's head began to pound again. She couldn't think of Sarah without remembering her nightmares.

"I'm going to try to see her after school, in case anybody wants to come with me," said Steve.

"I'll take you up on that," said Tasha.

"I'd like to come along, but I'm grounded," said Jennifer.

"I'll bet you are," said Tasha, giving her a sympathetic smile. "I'm going to go call my aunt again," she said, picking up her book bag.

Jennifer watched her leave. Secretly she was glad to have an excuse to avoid the hospital. She was afraid that seeing Sarah would make the nightmares worse. She shuddered as she pushed her lunch tray away and took out the lacquered pillbox her mother had given her for the aspirin. No one said anything as she swallowed the pills, and Jennifer couldn't help thinking that in fact no one seemed very concerned about her at all. Everyone was too busy worrying about Sarah.

When April approached their table, Steve got up suddenly and waved good-bye to everyone. Then Jennifer noticed that April was wearing her own pullover instead of one of Steve's oversized sweaters, which she had been borrowing for a week now. The two of them must have had a fight.

Cindy shot April a questioning look. April shook her head slightly and concentrated on her lunch.

"You two have an argument?" Cindy asked.

April picked up the empty juice cup from her tray

49

and scraped the waxy outside with a fingernail. "I don't want to talk about it."

"Come on," said Jennifer. "We're your friends."

April pointed at Kwame, who was reading a book at the end of the table. "Not in front of Kwame," she whispered. "He and Steve are close."

"Kwame, could you excuse us for a few minutes?" said Jennifer sweetly. She gave him a timid smile.

Cindy also flashed an apologetic smile. "It's a girl thing, Kwame."

He gallantly moved to a table halfway across the cafeteria. Cindy and Jennifer turned their attention back to April.

"We had a big fight. Something happened last night," April said quietly. Tears came to her eyes, but she blinked them back. "We were both stupid, and it got out of hand." Her friends leaned in close.

"Did you . . . uh, go all the way?" asked Jennifer.

"No, it's not that," said April. "We were at the West-cove Mall on Sunday picking up some pictures we had developed. When we got home, my parents were gone, but the answering machine was flashing. There was a message from Kwame telling me about Sarah. We went to the hospital, but they wouldn't let us see her. When we got back to my house, I was a wreck. Steve tried to comfort me, and . . ." April broke off.

"And?" chorused Cindy and Jennifer.

"That's when things got out of hand," said April. She realized she had torn the cup she had been fidgeting with. "I can't say any more," she said suddenly.

"It's too embarrassing."

"Don't leave us hanging," Cindy wailed.

"I'm sorry," April said firmly.

They kept insisting, but April held her ground. Whatever had happened, Cindy and Jennifer realized, they weren't going to find out from their friend.

When Steve approached Tasha at her locker after school, Cindy and José Melendez were with him.

"I don't know if they'll even let us in to see Sarah," Tasha warned them.

"We'll find out when we get there," said José, flipping his straight black hair away from his eyes. He had gone out with Sarah for a little while, and even though they hadn't worked out as a couple, they had remained good friends.

"I hate the fact that whoever did this to my cousin is still out there," said Tasha, slamming her locker shut.

"You mean you believe Jennifer's story about the truck?" said José, giving Tasha a surprised look.

"Why not?" said Tasha.

"Didn't you see the newspaper? The cops don't say anything about a truck," said José. "They say Jennifer lost control of her car."

"I wouldn't blame her for making something up," Steve added as they walked toward the student parking lot. "I mean, getting in an accident is bad enough, but putting your friend in the hospital . . . I think I'd try to pass the blame, too, especially if there weren't any witnesses to prove me wrong."

51

"That doesn't sound like Jennifer," said Tasha. But a cloud of doubt washed over her.

When Jennifer got home from school, there was a message on the answering machine to call Officer Edelman. She immediately called him back, ready to tell him how angry she was about the accident report in the paper.

"Why did you tell the newspaper that lie?" she demanded when he got on the line.

"I gave a version of the events that was based on the evidence," he said calmly. "We've been through this, Jennifer. But that's not why I called you. Your mom's insurance company wants a report on the accident. Do you have anything further to add to your account of the events?"

"What difference does it make?" Jennifer said rudely. "You'll just write down whatever you want."

"Not this time," he assured her. "And after I turn this in to the insurance company, I'll be out of your life forever. I promise. Now let's go over your description of the truck again."

She went through the questions with him. This time when the policeman asked her whether the truck had had any distinctive markings, something buzzed faintly in the back of her mind.

"Did the truck have hood ornaments on the grille?" the policeman asked. "A series of rings? A bulldog? A horse?" When he said, "A ram?" she hesitated, then finally said she couldn't remember.

"Did you believe me when I said I wasn't drunk or high on drugs?" Jennifer asked when the policeman had finished the questions.

"Yes," said Officer Edelman. "I did. And I believed you even more when I saw the results of the blood sample they took at the hospital. I have to go by evidence. If you come up with anything else, don't hesitate to call me at this number."

Jennifer hung up without saying good-bye.

18

Six

"That one's a fake," said Kwame, pointing to one of the paintings on the cafeteria wall. Bob Thornton, Tasha, and Jennifer swiveled around in their seats to get a better look.

The Murphy High administration was trying to brighten the atmosphere of the cafeteria. But instead of doing something important like improving the food, or getting rid of the huge spitballs on the ceiling, they had asked several students to hang their paintings on the wall. Now there was a contest going on to pick the best of the five paintings on display.

"Why, what do you mean, my dear boy?" asked Bob, pretending to hold a pipe as he did a Sherlock Holmes impression. He was one of Murphy High's most disruptive class clowns.

"I've seen that painting in an art book. Someone copied it," Kwame explained.

54

"Are you going to blow the whistle on the painter, Kwame?" asked Tasha.

"I'm not going to tattle," he said scornfully. "But I do think it's dishonest."

Jennifer looked at the picture they were talking about. It was a hunting scene. Two hunters were taking aim at a goat in the forest. Jennifer blinked. Actually, it wasn't a goat, it was a large buck. That's strange, she thought. Her heart started to beat faster. Why had she seen a goat at first? Did it have something to do with the accident? She stared at the buck to see whether the goat would come back into focus.

"Earth to Jennifer!" Bob held out an invisible microphone.

She looked back at the table and saw that they were all staring at her. "Something about the painting reminds me of the truck from the accident," she said slowly.

She caught José rolling his eyes. The rest of her friends looked away, embarrassed.

"You don't believe me, do you?" she asked them. It hurt even to ask the question. These were her best friends.

Steve looked at her sympathetically. "We were wondering," he began hesitantly. "Maybe when you passed out you, uh, you know, dreamed about the truck."

Jennifer was incredulous. "Is that what you all believe?" she demanded. Her friends stared blankly back at her. "Fine!" She pulled the chair back and took her tray across the room to a table that was just emptying.

e concentrated on her food, but now and then she peeked at the table she had left. Cindy and Tasha looked troubled, and she caught them glancing at her. When they waved to get her attention, she pretended she hadn't seen them.

Kwame took a roundabout way to the trash cans and stopped at her table. He sat down and waited for Jennifer to acknowledge him. Jennifer didn't. Finally he cleared his throat and said, "What did you see in the painting?"

"Forget it. It's stupid. Go back to your friends," said Jennifer tersely.

"It's not stupid if it's about the accident."

Jennifer looked into Kwame's eyes. They were warm and friendly, and he wanted to help her. She could see that. She took a deep breath. "This sounds so stupid, but I thought that deer in the picture was a goat for a second. I don't know why. I think it has to do with the truck."

"Maybe the truck was carrying goats or something. Maybe it had one of those hood ornaments shaped like a ram."

"I thought about the ram," Jennifer said. "But I don't think that's it. Besides," she added bitterly, "if I dreamed the whole thing, it doesn't matter."

"I believe you," said Kwame.

"You're sweet, Kwame," said Jennifer, "but I don't need your pity."

"I mean it," he said. "Nobody believes you because they think you're trying to avoid all the blame. Look," he said, pointing at her, "you weren't supposed to be out driving. You get into an accident and your friend gets hurt. So you make up a story about a truck hitting you so you can say it's not all your fault."

"I didn't make up the truck just to cover my butt!" said Jennifer. "But if there's no evidence . . ." She threw up her hands.

"I doubt that you would lie about something like this," said Kwame.

"Thanks, Kwame." Jennifer squeezed his arm. "You're a true friend."

"No charge," he said.

As he walked away, Jennifer had a flicker of remorse. How many times in the past had she called Kwame smart but immature, just because he was a year younger than everyone but April? Now he's the only one sticking by me, she realized.

Jennifer was lost in her thoughts when she climbed off the school bus. She didn't even hear the car horn honking until someone shouted her name. Jennifer looked up, still in a daze.

"Hey!" the voice called again.

This time Jennifer spotted Dave Hunter sitting in his car with the window rolled down.

"Oh, Dave. Sorry. I'm in my own world. You know, since the accident . . ."

"Can you go for a ride?" he asked.

"I can't. I'm grounded," Jennifer replied.

"Let me walk with you the rest of the way," said

Dave. He parked the car and fell into step with her on the sidewalk. He put his hands in the pockets of his long down jacket. "Have you gone to the hospital since the accident?" he asked her.

Jennifer shook her head.

"Me neither," he said.

She glanced at him, startled.

"I guess you're surprised, huh?" He kicked an acorn down the sidewalk and was quiet for a few minutes. "I can't handle hospitals." he said finally.

"I don't like them either," said Jennifer.

Dave went on as if he had not heard her. "I went to visit my grandfather this weekend. The last time I saw him was when my grandmother was dying. I went to see her and it seemed like everyone was dying in that place. I just can't handle hospitals."

You and me both, Jennifer thought. She watched him kick another acorn.

"Grandma looked so different, you know? They had her on painkillers and her mouth was hanging open like she was high. But even with the codeine, you could see she was in pain. I kept thinking, 'That's not Grandma.' I got back on Sunday night and heard about the accident. I felt really bad about not going straight over there. I felt even worse all day yesterday. I mean, she's my girlfriend. I should be there."

"I know what you mean," said Jennifer. "My mom would lift my curfew if I wanted to visit her. But I saw her for five minutes and it's like you said about your grandmother: That's not Sarah." She turned away so that he wouldn't see her tears. "I'm sorry about the accident, Dave. I know how you feel about Sarah."

"Hey, it was an accident. I know you feel guilty about it. I feel guilty about not visiting her. But I don't blame you."

"I've been having these terrible nightmares about it ever since it happened." Jennifer told him about the tubes and the wires, and the look on Sarah's face.

They had reached Jennifer's driveway. When she first saw the strange car parked there, Jennifer thought they had company. Then she remembered that her mother had gotten a loaner car from the insurance company. What's Mom doing home from work already? Jennifer wondered.

"Look, I'd better get inside."

"Okay. Thanks for hearing me out. I had to tell somebody, and I figured you would understand." He gave her a hug before he left.

Her mother was standing by the kitchen door when she walked in. "Was that Dave Hunter out there with you? Didn't I tell you to come straight home every day after school?"

"Mom . . ."

"Don't 'Mom' me!" said Mrs. Wilson sternly. "You have a curfew and you'd better stick to it, young lady."

"He walked me home from the bus stop, that's all." Jennifer dropped her book bag on the kitchen floor and opened the refrigerator. "He wanted to talk about Sarah."

"Did you ride in his car?" Mrs. Wilson asked.

"I told you, he walked me from the bus stop," said Jennifer.

"Okay," Mrs. Wilson said. "But from now on, if you want to drive anywhere, you drive with me, or ride the bus, is that clear? I'm sure Dave Hunter is a very good driver, but I forbid you to get into a car with anyone from school. That includes Dave Hunter and your other friends."

Jennifer just nodded. How could she tell her mother that after today she didn't have any other friends anyway?

Jennifer tried doing homework, but it was no use. All she could think about was Sarah lying in the hospital and the argument she'd had with her friends. Jennifer had never felt so lonely in her life. Finally she picked up the phone and dialed Tasha's number. Immediately the other girl apologized.

"Listen, Jennifer, I'm really sorry about what happened today," Tasha said. "We're all really tense. I totally believe you when you say there was a truck involved."

Jennifer felt much better after talking with Tasha. She called Cindy next, who also apologized and said she thought their energy would be better spent trying to help Sarah. Jennifer agreed and was making plans to meet Cindy at school tomorrow when her mother knocked once and stuck her head in the doorway of Jennifer's room.

"Are you on the phone, honey?" her mother said.

"I'll come back later."

Jennifer gestured for her mother to come in. Then she said a quick good-bye to Cindy and hung up the phone.

Mrs. Wilson was holding the note that Jennifer had slipped into one of her portfolios. "Thanks," she said, waving the note. She picked up a dress from the floor and folded it absentmindedly as she spoke. "I wanted to tell you why I don't want you riding in other people's cars," she said. "When Robert and I landed in Chicago, I heard myself being paged in the airport. Right then, I knew something terrible had happened to you. I turned to Robert and said, 'Jennifer's hurt.' When Cherise told me you were in the hospital, I almost fainted right there." Mrs. Wilson blinked hard. She reached across the desk for a tissue as her eyes began to tear. "When I talked to Mrs. Gordon, she told me you were all right, but I had to come home. You'll never know the hell I went through on the flight back. All I could say, over and over, was 'My baby, my baby.'"

Jennifer felt her own tears coming on as she watched her mother wipe her eyes.

"I don't want you to think I'm being cruel to you," Mrs. Wilson said softly. "But until I get over this feeling, I want you here after school. Near me, okay? I can't imagine what Sarah's mother and father are going through. But it could have been you, and I—" Mrs. Wilson broke off in midsentence and pressed her fist to her mouth.

Jennifer hugged her mother. Mrs. Wilson held her tightly for a long time. Finally she took a deep breath. "I'll let you alone now," she said, giving Jennifer a kiss. "Don't forget we have that appointment with Windjammer Insurance tomorrow. We need to find out how the accident affects my policy. Your permit may be revoked, you know."

Jennifer sighed. "I know."

An hour later Jennifer turned off the light and climbed into bed. It's all my fault, she thought. Because of me, Mom is miserable. Because of me, Sarah is in a coma. As she closed her eyes the image of a goat floated into her mind. It was gone as quickly as it appeared. Jennifer's heart beat faster. Once again she had the feeling that the image was somehow connected to the accident.

Jennifer wore jeans and a black sweater to school the next day. Usually she loved to dress up for school, but since the accident on Saturday she hadn't wanted to call attention to herself. She didn't even care that her eyes were red and puffy.

When Jennifer met Tasha at her locker, she noticed the tension in her friend's face, too. Tasha was very irritable, and she'd stopped doing her hair. It had been in the same ponytail for three days.

When will this end? Jennifer wondered. How long can we all go through this?

After school Jennifer got her books and headed out the door. Mrs. Wilson was waiting in her car at the curb.

Jennifer climbed in and gave her mother a quick kiss.

Windjammer Insurance was in the suburbs west of Madison. Mrs. Wilson felt strongly about giving her business to black-owned enterprises, and Windjammer was owned and run by a black couple. When they got there, they were told that their agent, Kellis Monroe, wouldn't be available because of an emergency. The receptionist led them to a different office. Emerson Plint was the name stenciled on the door.

Jennifer was not impressed by Mr. Plint. He had steel-rimmed glasses and was bald on both sides of his head. On the top of his head were little tufts of hair arranged in neat rows. Implants, Jennifer observed. He wore a brown jacket that looked as if it had been the height of fashion thirty years ago. And when Jennifer noticed his wedding ring, she couldn't help thinking, There's someone for everyone.

"Come in, Mrs. Wilson," Mr. Plint said in a flat voice. He didn't even look at Jennifer.

The office was covered with plants of every size. A row of cacti lined the front of his desk, and ferns hung from the window behind his chair. The tops of his files were draped with ivy and spider plants. Mrs. Wilson ducked under the branch of a spreading fichus tree and took the only seat available.

"Sorry about the one chair," Emerson Plint said with a sneer. "I don't have room for two."

You would if you mowed your office! Jennifer thought.

Mr. Plint looked over the documents on his desk.

"Let's see," he said slowly. "On Saturday your daughter took your car to the mall with Sarah Gordon. While turning left on Dawes Highway, she lost control of the vehicle and spun into a steamroller that was parked at a construction site."

"That's not true!" Jennifer cried. "I was hit by a truck."

Mr. Plint folded his hands. "I don't see that information in the police report."

"They don't believe me, but that's what happened," said Jennifer. Kwame was right, she realized; there were a lot of reasons why people thought she was lying.

"Is this the car?" Mr. Plint asked. He flipped a Polaroid picture around so that Mrs. Wilson could see it. Jennifer recognized the back of the Saab, but the front end looked like a crumpled piece of red paper. Jennifer shuddered as the accident replayed in her mind.

"I talked to our claims adjuster," said Mr. Plint. "He didn't see any evidence of a truck."

"But—" Jennifer began.

"And," Mr. Plint interrupted loudly, "there were no skid marks or other evidence of any kind." He softened his tone when he saw the challenging look on Mrs. Wilson's face. "You see, I have to go by what the claims adjuster says to get the company to settle your claim."

"Doesn't what I say count for anything?" Jennifer cried.

"Yes, that's why you're here," said Mr. Plint. He

handed Jennifer a sheet of paper and pointed to the top. "Here is where you can put down *your* version of the events. You can even draw an overhead picture of the accident in this box here. In the meantime," he added briskly as he handed her a pen, "I would like to discuss some matters with your mother."

Jennifer took the paper to the reception area and hunched over the coffee table to write a complete description. She left out the fact that she wasn't supposed to be driving, since it didn't have anything to do with the accident. When she had finished drawing her car and the truck in the little box, she returned to Mr. Plint's office. She tried not to look at Mr. Plint when she handed him the paper. He put it back in the folder without looking at it.

Mrs. Wilson was in a bad mood all the way home. "You may have jeopardized my insurance policy, and there may be legal ramifications to your driving without an adult," she said sternly. "And on top of that, they say the accident was your fault."

"But it wasn't," said Jennifer wearily.

"I know," said Mrs. Wilson. But this time even she sounded doubtful.

Seven

"Great day for a fire drill," said Billy Turner miserably.

Tasha nodded. Rain pelted the crowd of students returning to the building. Inside Tasha spied Cindy standing a few feet from the main office. She was talking in hushed tones to a trio of sophomore girls. "I'll catch up with you later, Billy," said Tasha. She hurried over to Cindy.

"April's been acting weird lately," one of the sophomore girls was saying. "She doesn't hang out after classes anymore and she hasn't returned any of my phone calls."

"Yeah," a blonde chimed in. "And what's up with her and Steve?"

Cindy shook her head. "Something happened between her and Steve. I'm really worried about it. I think he took advantage of her while he was comforting her."

66

"You're jumping to conclusions," Tasha said. "Steve's a good guy."

"What happens if he did take advantage of her?" asked the sophomore who was wearing glasses. "Is that considered sexual assault?"

Cindy nodded. "It sure is. And if I find out something like that happened between them, I'll report it to the principal. Guys can't get away with stuff like that—April could even charge him with sexual assault."

One of April's classmates looked horrified. "Maybe I could write a note to April so she'll know she's not alone," she said.

"Whoa!" Tasha cried. "You better make sure Steve did something first. I, for one, highly doubt it."

"What else could be going on?" the girl with the glasses challenged. "April herself said they got carried away."

Tasha waved her hand impatiently. "Maybe they fought over what movie to see, or who should pay for dinner. There are lots of things people fight about. Sarah and I argue about the dumbest things." Tasha's breath caught slightly. "Anyway," she added quickly, "just make sure you're right before you call Steve a rapist."

"You sound as if you want him to get away with it," said the girl with glasses.

"Get away with what?" Tasha snapped. "Look, I like April as much as you do, but if she's upset about something, it's her responsibility to tell a grown-up. . . ."

The rest of the words died in Tasha's throat. April was approaching them.

"Hi," said Cindy brightly. "What's up?"

April eyed her friends curiously. "What's up with you?"

"Nothing," Tasha replied, glaring at the other four girls. "We were just talking about how nasty rumors get started."

"Jennifer," Tasha said impatiently, "we're going to the hospital—not the prom. If you don't hurry up, we'll have to take the city bus. All the school buses are about to leave."

Jennifer looked up and noticed that she and Tasha were the only two people left in the hallway. At lunch Tasha had announced that she was going to the hospital to bring a bunch of get-well cards from people in school. She had asked whether anybody wanted to come, and before Jennifer knew what she was doing she found herself saying yes. And when Jennifer called her mother at work to see whether it was okay, Mrs. Wilson had said yes. Jennifer almost wished her mother had said no instead. Seeing Sarah again would be one of the hardest things she'd ever done.

Jennifer followed Tasha aboard a school bus that stopped near the hospital. Tasha balanced a paper shopping bag on her lap. Inside were dozens of get-well cards and folded pieces of notebook paper from the students at Murphy. The news about Sarah was encouraging. She had been moved from the Head

Trauma Unit to a suite on the same floor. "It means her condition is stable," Tasha told Jennifer hopefully, "but she's still in a coma."

Jennifer was glad to hear some better news, but she was still distraught over Sarah. What if she didn't recover? And Jennifer knew that Cindy, Tasha, and Kwame believed she hadn't caused the accident, but most of the students at Murphy openly suspected that the story about the truck had been Jennifer's way of avoiding the blame. One girl in her English class particularly irked her. Before, she had said hello to Jennifer every day because Jennifer was popular and knew a lot of boys. But today when Jennifer had smiled at her, the girl had looked away.

The school bus rumbled through Madison's business district. The sun suddenly broke through the rain clouds that had soaked the Murphy High students during the fire drill. Jennifer looked out at several car dealerships and insurance offices. She was noticing them everywhere since the accident—police cars, too. Finally the bus stopped at an apartment complex down the road from Madison County Hospital and Tasha grabbed her bag. Jennifer trailed after her.

Inside the hospital Tasha and Jennifer signed the visitors' log, and the nurse directed them to an elevator down the hall. The smell of flowers mingled with the disinfectant emanating from a bucket a janitor was using to mop the floor. Jennifer peeked inside an open door. A man lay on the bed playing a hand-held video game. The hall to the children's ward was visible, and they saw a clown tying balloons into funny shapes for a crowd of kids in hospital gowns.

They walked down the blue hallway, past the doors marked "Head Trauma Unit," to a series of nearby wards.

"Room One-Oh-Three," Tasha said, stopping at a door. "This is it."

At first Jennifer and Tasha thought they were in the wrong room. When they walked in, they saw a pale white girl with thick black-rimmed glasses staring at them. Her bed had been cranked up so that she could read comfortably. She waved at them with her magazine and then pointed to Tasha's bag. "Is that for me? You shouldn't have."

Jennifer and Tasha smiled. "Come on in," the girl said." "You must be looking for my roommate. Sarah's over there." She pointed to the other bed that was behind a pleated partition.

Jennifer's heart began to beat faster as Tasha pushed aside the divider.

There was a window on Sarah's side, and that was where Jennifer directed her eyes. The whole city of Madison was visible on the other side of the river. She stared at the cars speeding along the highway that bordered the river.

"Would you mind leaving the divider open?" asked the other patient. "I like the light from the window. By the way, my name is Carla."

"What happened to you?" Jennifer asked, relieved to be able to look away from Sarah's side of the room.

"Spinal operation," Carla said. "I'll spare you the gory details." She made a face.

Tasha said hello to Sarah and then started setting up the get-well cards along the windowsill. Jennifer went over and helped her prop them up.

"You can put them on the heating vent over here if you need the room," Carla offered.

When all the cards were set up, the room seemed much more colorful. Tasha had saved the largest card for last. She tore off a piece of the masking tape she had brought with her and stuck it to the back of a drawing of Sarah.

"That's really good. Did you do that?" Carla asked.

Tasha nodded. She leaned over the machine that monitored her cousin's heartbeat and pressed the drawing to the wall. "No thumbtacks, cuz," she said with a sad smile.

A moment later Tasha began sniffling, but Jennifer didn't dare look in her direction.

They all turned toward the door when they heard a knock. A portly black man in his fifties entered. He wore a dark blue suit and polished brown shoes, and he carried a thick black book and a hat in the same hand.

"Good afternoon," he said in a clear baritone voice. He looked across the room. "Is that Ms. Sarah Gordon?" he asked as he approached the bed.

"Who are you?" asked Tasha.

"I'm Leonard Bale, the pastor at Mount Zion Baptist," he said politely. "Dave Hunter's mother goes to my church and she asked me to stop in on Sarah Gor-

71

don the next time I was visiting folks here."

Reverend Bale put his hat on the hook behind the door and opened his Bible. "Would you girls like to join me in a short prayer?"

Jennifer nodded and bowed her head. She saw Carla bowing hers as well.

"The Lord is my shepherd, I shall not want," Reverend Bale began.

Tasha suddenly crumpled the paper bag, picked up her coat, and ran out of the room. She slammed the door behind her, knocking the reverend's hat to the floor.

If he was upset by Tasha's behavior, he didn't show it. He finished the Twenty-third Psalm and began another prayer. Jennifer didn't know what to do. The reverend had his eyes closed, and his head was bowed.

Jennifer turned away from the reverend and looked out the window. Below she could see Tasha walking across the parking lot toward the river. As Jennifer watched, Tasha swung her legs over the low railing and dropped onto a narrow ledge below that separated the jogging path from the huge concrete blocks that bordered the water on both sides. Jennifer gasped when she saw Tasha climb one of the blocks and then disappear down the other side.

Eight

Jennifer rushed past Reverend Bale and out of the room. The nearest exit led to a flight of stairs. She took them two at a time. At the bottom a sign announced that an alarm would ring if the door was opened. She debated opening it. Then she noticed it was propped open. She pushed on it and it swung out without tripping the alarm.

Jennifer sprinted across the parking lot and climbed over the low railing. "Tasha! Where are you!" she cried. She didn't get an answer. Then she saw Tasha below, near the water's edge. She was crouched down, clutching her knees and sobbing loudly.

Jennifer carefully let herself down the jagged slope until she reached her friend. "Tasha," she said gently, "Sarah's going to be all right. I know she will." She reached out to touch her friend, but Tasha moved away from her hand. Jennifer sat down, deciding to give

Tasha some room to talk, if that was what she wanted to do.

"I hate hospitals!" Tasha exclaimed. She looked exhausted from crying. "When my parents were in the hospital, I went to see them, but they were already gone. The doctor told me they died without regaining consciousness, so they didn't suffer. Afterwards, I wanted to kill myself. I couldn't take the pain." Fresh tears came to her eyes.

First her parents were in an accident, and now her cousin, Jennifer thought. She listened as Tasha described the depression that had lasted for months after the funeral. "I cried myself to sleep for months and I barely ate," Tasha said. "I can't tell you what it's like to have your parents taken away like that."

Jennifer thought about the ten months before her parents had finally decided to get divorced. She, too, had cried herself to sleep, drowning out the sounds of her parents' fights. The pain she endured during her parents' separation and divorce was something she had never talked about with anyone. She looked over at Tasha now. "I don't know what it's like to have your parents die," she admitted, "but I do remember how hard it was when my parents split up."

Tasha looked into her eyes as Jennifer continued. "I'd do anything to have the kind of family life that you and Sarah have. I can't tell you how many times I've been jealous of the two of you." Her voice cracked, and then she began sobbing. "I'm so sorry, Tasha. This is all my fault."

Tasha reached out to hug Jennifer, and the two of them were standing that way when the sound of unsteady footsteps came from the other side of the concrete block. Tasha and Jennifer both looked up and saw Reverend Bale trying to keep his balance as he lowered himself with one hand, holding his Bible in the other.

"You two okay down here? You scared me and Carla to bits," he said.

"We'll be all right," Jennifer told him.

"What about you?" he asked Tasha softly.

Tasha glanced up at him and nodded briefly.

Reverend Bale's eyebrows shot up. "Is the girl in the other bed your sister?"

Tasha didn't answer. She stared at the water.

"They're cousins," Jennifer explained.

"It doesn't work!" Tasha shouted abruptly. She whirled around to face the minister. Reverend Bale looked taken aback.

"What doesn't work, child?" he said.

"Your prayers," Tasha said hotly. "I should know. I prayed for my parents not to die, but they did."

"I see," said the reverend. For a moment no one spoke. Finally he said, "When your parents didn't live, did you ask for the strength to carry on?"

"I prayed for them to live! And it didn't work. And now Sarah is up there dying and no praying is going to help her either."

The reverend was silent for a moment. Then he said to Tasha, "Carla told me you made that drawing of Sarah that's in the room. You've got a lot of talent and

75

energy—I have a feeling your cousin can sense your presence, Tasha. Maybe that will be of some comfort to you."

He didn't wait for a response. Instead he nodded good-bye and turned back to the hospital.

"Do you want to be alone?" Jennifer whispered to Tasha.

Tasha shook her head. "No. Let's go." Together they walked back to the main entrance of the hospital. A receptionist told them that visiting hours were over.

"But I left my book bag in there," Jennifer said. The receptionist gave her a stern look and motioned for them to go ahead.

Carla was sitting up on the bed when they walked in. Her dinner tray was propped up over her lap and she waved to them with her fork. "Hey, you're back. I was hoping that nothing had happened to you." She dug the fork into the poached chicken and popped it in her mouth. "Oh!" she cried. "I almost forgot. The doctor came in while you were gone. He thinks Sarah may be coming out of it pretty soon. Her brain waves are different."

Tasha looked excited. "How soon?" she asked.

"I don't know," Carla admitted. "When you've been in and out of hospitals like I have, you figure out 'pretty soon' could mean anything."

"How do you stand it?" said Jennifer. "I mean, cooped up in here day after day. Don't you get depressed?"

Carla nodded. "I guess," she said. "I try not to think

76

about it too much, you know? I try to take it day by day." She dug into the applesauce. "When you were gone, I counted the cards around the room: ninety-three! Sarah must be Homecoming Queen or something."

"She gets along with practically everybody," said Tasha. "Do you go to Murphy?"

"Used to," said Carla. "But I missed so many days, I couldn't keep up. They switched me to Hamilton High. It's not as bad as everybody says."

"Her uncle is the principal there," said Jennifer, pointing at Tasha.

"Yeah, I know. He was in here yesterday," said Carla. "We talked for a long time." She looked at Tasha.

"I'd better go before my mom gets worried," said Jennifer, putting her book bag on her shoulder. She waited outside while Tasha went over to say good-bye to Sarah. Jennifer still couldn't deal with the sight of her friend.

There were no lights on when Jennifer got home. She clicked on the answering machine and heard her mother's voice. "Hi, baby, it's me. It was nice of you to go see Sarah. Robert and I will be home by around seven. There's some chicken in the fridge. And could you make a salad? Love you."

Jennifer was finishing the salad preparations when her mother came in. The talk she and Tasha had had was still in her mind as she gave her mother an especially tight hug.

Mrs. Wilson's coat smelled of cold night air and perfume. "Whew, you're glad to see me!" she said. She looked at her daughter with mock suspicion. "What have you been up to?"

Jennifer shrugged. "I just love you. I'm glad you're my mother," she said, and she meant every word.

Nine

"Any new ideas?" Mr. Harris asked Jennifer, Cindy, Kwame, and José. They were sitting in the back of 18 Pine St. It took a second for the Murphy High gang to figure out that he was talking about suggestions for his latest pizza.

"I have a great one," said José. "*El Magnifico*. It means the Magnificent One."

Mr. Harris looked around the table. "Any others?" he said hopefully.

"Give me a minute," said José, undeterred. He took a piece of paper out of his pocket. "How about the Fantastic Four? The Meatpie? Chewlicious? The Widowmaker? The Manly Mouthful?"

The girls booed the last suggestion.

"Keep trying," said Mr. Harris kindly as he headed back to the counter.

79

Jennifer had trouble keeping up with the conversation. She was breaking her curfew, which was making her feel worried. And she was exhausted. For the fifth day in a row, she was running on only two or three hours of sleep. But Kwame had left a note in her locker which said, "Good news about the truck, I might have a clue." Jennifer had decided to meet him at 18 Pine, even if it meant making her mother furious. She had to find out what he'd discovered.

As soon as Kwame finished eating, he crumpled his napkin and threw it on the plate. He stood up and motioned Jennifer over to an empty booth.

"Oooh, Kwame and Jennifer want some privacy," said Cindy. "This ought to be good."

"Go for it, Kwame," said José, raising his soda cup.

Jennifer ignored them, but Kwame shot José a disgusted look. He opened his notebook and showed Jennifer a sketch he had drawn of the Murphy High building and grounds.

"Kwame, what is this?" said Jennifer.

Kwame pointed to the top of the sketch. "Here's the main entrance, and here are the playing fields. You know these woods over here?"

Jennifer nodded. The "woods" was just a clump of trees and bushes in a corner of the high school property. A group of tough white kids used the area to sneak cigarettes during recess. And sometimes kids cut through the trees and climbed over a low fence to get to a gas station where you could buy soda and other snacks.

"I was out in the playing fields during lunch," Kwame said, "and I noticed a guy smoking near those woods. He had a bandage over his nose, and he was limping a little. He was looking at me, and I asked Rob Delaney who he was. Rob told me that he didn't know much about him except that his name was Jim Gardiner and he thought he heard him bragging on Tuesday about being in a car accident."

"So?" Jennifer prodded him.

"So, I asked around. One of his teachers told me that he said he broke his nose over the weekend in a fight with his older brother."

Jennifer stared at Kwame.

Kwame looked into her eyes. "Jim Gardiner lied to that teacher. Why? If the accident happened the way you've described it, he could have banged his nose on his steering wheel when he hit your car."

Jennifer shook her head. "Look, Kwame, I appreciate it, but this doesn't do me much good."

"I'm going to investigate further," he insisted.

"Maybe Jim really did have a fight with his brother and didn't want his friends to know he got beat up." Jennifer put a hand on her friend's arm. "Thank you," she said softly. "I really do appreciate all you've done, but we don't have enough proof. It doesn't matter anyway, because almost no one believes my story." Jennifer looked at her friends talking at the next table. "*I'm* even starting to wonder—maybe I did imagine the truck!"

"There's one other thing I wanted to show you."

81

Kwame pulled out a copy of a football schedule. On the top corner was a cartoon drawing of Wally the Goat, Murphy High's mascot. "Could this be the goat you've pictured? The senior T-shirt has Wally's picture on it. Maybe that's what you saw."

Jennifer looked at it for a moment . "I don't think so. I keep seeing a real-looking goat, not a cartoon drawing."

Kwame closed his notebook. "Well, I'm out of ideas. I thought I was onto something with that kid with the broken nose." He took out a plastic sandwich bag from his backpack and showed it to Jennifer. "At least I didn't waste my whole lunch hour. I found these."

Inside the bag were two four-leaf clovers.

"For Sarah," he explained. "I'm going to bring them to her for good luck."

When they returned to the table, Dave Hunter was also there. He looks like he hasn't had much sleep these days, either, Jennifer thought. As far as she knew, he still hadn't been to see Sarah. He nodded a greeting at Jennifer.

"My mom told me you met the famous Reverend Bale," he said with a smile. "I figured if anybody could bring Sarah out of it, he could."

Cindy shook her head and sighed. "It's so weird, you know? It's like Sarah's in a trance. She's not getting worse; she's not getting better."

"I wonder if she dreams," said Kwame.

Jennifer shuddered.

Dave looked at his fingers as he tapped the table absentmindedly. "I saw this story on the news about a kid who was in a coma, and nothing could bring him out of it. Then, one day, his parents brought the dog to the kid's room. When the dog barked, the kid woke up. Just like that."

"That sounds a little farfetched," said Cindy.

"No, I saw the same news story," said Kwame.

"The thing is, Sarah doesn't have a dog. And all her friends and family members have been talking to her," José pointed out.

Dave squirmed in his seat.

Jennifer stood up. She had to get home. Her mother would be home from work any minute.

There were no cars in the driveway when Jennifer hurried to the door. She tossed her book bag on the floor and sprawled on the white sofa to catch her breath. The phone rang, and she let it ring two more times while she composed herself. She picked up the phone, expecting her mother.

It was Steve Adams. His voice sounded pinched.

"Can someone tell me what's going on?" he demanded. When Jennifer asked him to explain, he laughed bitterly. "You mean you haven't heard?"

"No," said Jennifer. "What are you talking about?"

"April and I had a fight, that's all, and now there are rumors all over school. Today I got a piece of hate mail." He told her that someone had deposited a folded piece of paper with a drawing of a creepy-looking guy in a trench coat in his locker. Steve's name was written above the drawing.

Jennifer couldn't believe it. She'd been so preoccupied with Sarah and her own problems that she didn't know what was going on at Murphy this week. The two times that April had avoided her at school, Jennifer had assumed that it was because of the accident.

"Look," she said, "as far as I know, everybody has a different idea about why you two broke up. Last I heard April wasn't talking about what happened, so people must be thinking the worst."

"Why do *you* think we broke up?" Steve demanded.

"I don't know. I just assumed you had a misunderstanding. I thought you'd be back together by now—I know how much you two like each other."

There was a pause on the line.

"It's no one's business," said Steve harshly. "But meanwhile I'm the bad guy, and April is the innocent victim. Today everybody ignored me at lunch, did you notice that? They all sat at the other end of the table."

Actually Jennifer had noticed that much. She didn't know what to say.

"If these are the kinds of friends I have," said Steve, "I'm glad I know it now!" He hung up.

Jennifer held the receiver for a minute, then dialed Cindy's number, hoping she'd be back from 18 Pine St. She wasn't. They were probably all still there, having a good time without Jennifer.

As Jennifer headed back upstairs, she realized that Steve and she were in exactly the same boat. Unless she could prove her innocence—prove that she hadn't caused the accident that put Sarah in the coma—she would be spending a lot of time by herself.

Ten

Jennifer saw the green arrow, put on her left-turn signal, and pulled out onto Dawes Highway. She looked to the left and saw nobody coming. She was already turning the wheel when she finally glanced to the right. Sarah's face was as white as a ghost's, and a truck was barreling toward them. This time she was already covered with tubes and patches. She clawed desperately at Jennifer as the truck slammed into them.

When Jennifer woke up, wet and shivering from her own sweat, her clock read 12:08. She got up and went to the bathroom and washed her face. She didn't feel like lying down again, so she grabbed her bathrobe from the hook behind her door and headed for the kitchen. She poured a glass of milk and stared at the wallpaper.

She had stood against that same wall when her

mother snapped a picture of her before Colin Greenleaf had come to take her to the sophomore dance last year. He had been a senior then, and now he played football for Dominic College. Jennifer's stomach tightened when it occurred to her that Sarah might never go to another dance.

Jennifer closed her eyes, forcing herself to think of something else. She imagined the Caribbean dance, picturing herself in a gorgeous hot-pink dress dancing with a handsome guy from her math class, and then saw Sarah standing with Dave in front of the school, crowned the Caribbean Queen. Tears gathered in Jennifer's eyes and suddenly the accident began to play back again. Jennifer immediately open her eyes, trying to stop the nightmare.

All at once Jennifer knew what she had to do. She quietly returned to her room, dressed quickly, rearranged the pillows and sheets, and went back down to the kitchen. She took the phone book from the drawer in the counter, picked up the phone, and made a call. Then she took her coat and crept soundlessly to the white sofa in the living room to wait.

A car drove slowly down the street; the driver was checking the numbers on the doors. Jennifer got up and walked to the front door. The driver had found the house and was idling on the street. Jennifer prayed he wouldn't honk his horn.

"To the hospital," she said once she was inside the taxi. The driver nodded and slipped the car into gear. He was a dark man with a heavy mustache. He didn't seem curious about why a sixteen-year-old would be sneaking out of the house in the middle of the night. He drove silently as Jennifer looked out the windshield at the quiet city. The streetlamps lit the brick buildings downtown with a hazy orange color.

The driver lit a cigarette with one hand and rolled down his window. The radio was tuned in to a talk show. A woman with a whiny voice was explaining to a man why his statements were racist. Tension seemed to fill the air. Jennifer was about to tell the driver to turn around and go home when the hospital loomed into view. Most of the windows were dark. Streetlamps illuminated the empty visitors' parking lot. Jennifer heard a siren and saw flashing lights reflecting off the taxi's windshield. She turned around to see an ambulance driving past them. The ambulance kept its siren on all the way to the emergency entrance.

Jennifer asked the driver to stop by the main doors. She paid him and climbed out. Through the glass doors she could see a receptionist at the front desk. She was chatting on the phone while a security guard read a newspaper at a desk near the door. Jennifer knew she would never get past the security guard or the receptionist, but she hoped they wouldn't even see her.

Once the driver left Jennifer made her way toward the back of the building. As she passed the brightly lit emergency wing, where the ambulance was still idling, she kept her head down.

Finally she reached the doctors' parking lot and the door where she had exited yesterday when Tasha had run down to the river. This time it wouldn't budge. She gripped the door handle and pulled with all her strength.

"Yes," Jennifer cried triumphantly as the door swung open. She slipped inside. Her heart was pounding so hard, she had to gulp a few times to slow her breathing and keep in control. The stairwell was well lit. As she climbed the stairs, she could hear the building's furnace humming from somewhere behind the cinder-block walls.

The door to Sarah and Carla's room was unlocked. Jennifer pushed the handle and opened it a fraction of an inch at a time. She heard soft radio music coming from the nurses' station down the hall.

Carla was snoring in the near bed. Tiptoeing past her, Jennifer made her way to the other side of the room. Her eyes were becoming accustomed to the dark, and she could make out Sarah's form in the other bed. The metal rails around the bed were locked in place; Sarah looked as if she were sleeping in a crib.

Jennifer held her breath as she reached over the rail and grabbed her friend's still hand. It was cool.

Jennifer almost felt surprised when Sarah's eyes didn't flutter open and stare at Jennifer with rage. Sarah wasn't half-deformed as she had appeared in the dream. Her head was resting on the white pillow, her lips slightly parted as she breathed. The heart monitor behind her shot a constant jagged line across the screen. Jennifer blinked, and a tear ran down her cheek.

"Sarah," Jennifer whispered. "If you can hear me, I want you to know I'm sorry. I was wrong about taking the car; we should have let your grandmother take us to the mall. Which reminds me, we still have to find dresses for the dance, so get better, okay?"

There was no response. Carla's gentle snoring was the only sound. The heart monitor continued its monotonous green flickering. Jennifer stood over Sarah until her back began to ache. She gave Sarah's hand a final squeeze. "You're going to make it," she whispered.

At first she thought the noise was Carla stirring. Then she realized the sound she heard was footsteps. The footsteps stopped. She looked across the room and realized with horror that the door was being opened.

Eleven

Holding her breath, Jennifer tiptoed frantically into the bathroom. It must be a security guard. She slipped behind the door and held her coat around her body so that it wouldn't rustle. Her heart was beating so wildly, her whole body seemed to be pulsing. She let out her breath as quietly as possible, and waited.

From the crack in the open door, Jennifer saw him step into the room. He had on dark pants and a jacket. He stayed by the door for a second, looking intently at Carla. Then he crossed over to Sarah's bed and paused. What if he checks the bathroom? Jennifer thought. She imagined the look on the security guard's face as she explained about the sleepless nights and the night-mares she'd been having and how she'd finally had to come and see Sarah. She doubted that that would make a difference to the guard.

Then Jennifer heard the male voice whispering,

"You're going to be okay." Jennifer thought the voice sounded familiar. "You'll pull through, I promise. Okay, baby? I love you."

There was a pause as his voice broke. Jennifer strained to hear more. But he was speaking too softly.

Carla suddenly stopped snoring. She shifted around in her bed and then Jennifer heard a cry of panic escape from her throat. "What are you doing in here?" she whispered. "Get out!" she said loudly.

"I'm a friend of Sarah's," the intruder said.

Dave Hunter! Jennifer wanted to run out and hug him. But, embarrassed by her hidden position, she retreated into the shadows of the bathroom as Carla turned on the light near her bed.

"Visiting hours are over," said Carla grumpily. "What are you doing here at this hour?" she demanded.

"My name is Dave Hunter," Dave began. "I'm Sarah Gordon's boyfriend—"

"Oh yeah?" Carla interrupted. "Then how come I've never seen you here?"

"This is the first time I've come," said Dave. Jennifer could hear the shame in his voice. "I couldn't handle it. Then I started to feel so bad—I couldn't eat, I couldn't sleep. So I drove down here. My mom used to do some volunteer work at the hospital. I know a lot of nurses from picking her up afterward. That's how come they let me in. I didn't mean to wake you," said Dave.

"That's okay," said Carla. The frightened tone was gone. Dave had that effect on most women, Jennifer thought. "How come you didn't wait until tomorrow?"

"I couldn't sleep. And besides, I had this idea." Dave told her the news story about the boy who had recovered when he heard his dog barking. "I was the only person she hadn't heard," he said. "I know it sounds stupid," he added, "but I thought she might wake up if she heard my voice tonight."

"I think it sounds wonderful," Carla said warmly. "You must really love her, Dave."

"Yeah, I guess so."

" 'I guess so' my foot!" Carla cried. "You're a *mensch*!"

"A what?"

"A *mensch*. It's Yiddish," she explained. "It means a good guy—sensitive. You're not afraid to let your feelings show."

Dave laughed softly. "I don't know. It's easy to say 'I love you' to your girlfriend when she's unconscious."

"Why don't you wake her up?" said Carla. "Did you try the Sleeping Beauty treatment?"

"You know, I was thinking about that," admitted Dave.

"It couldn't hurt," Carla prompted.

"Naw, that's silly," Dave said. "I'd better get going."

"Suit yourself," said Carla. "Of course, you're going to drive all the way home wondering if you could have revived the woman you love with a kiss. . . . Oh well, it was just a thought." She turned off the fluorescent light and settled herself into bed.

93

"All right," said Dave. "You made your point."

Jennifer heard the railing on Sarah's bed clank slightly as Dave leaned over and kissed her gently on the lips.

"I love you, Sarah," he said softly. "Hey, look at the machine," he said, nearly shouting. "The heartbeat just went from sixty-eight to ninety-one!"

"This is it!" said Carla. Jennifer peered around the door. Carla's excited expression slowly faded. Anxiety replaced it.

"It's going down again," Dave said. A long moment passed. "Now it's down to sixty-four beats per minute; that's slower than when I started," he said.

Carla clucked sympathetically as Dave crossed to the door. "I'm glad you gave it a try, Dave. And you're still a *mensch*. I hope you don't mind if I tell her about it when she comes to."

"You mean *if* she comes to, don't you?" Dave murmured.

"She'll come out of it," Carla assured him. "Trust me. I've been in and out of hospitals since I was five. You pick up a few things. The doctors around here aren't really expecting the worst. They're surprised she's been out this long, but they expect her to snap out of it any day now."

"I hope so. Wouldn't it have been great if it had worked?"

"Awesome," Carla admitted. Dave gave her a hug.

Jennifer decided to walk out. More than anyone else, Dave would be able to understand why she was there as well. He would accept her guilt about Sarah without adding to it. And, Jennifer thought, he could drive me home. Before she could take a step, however, the door to the room opened and Jennifer heard a nurse's voice.

"Dave, I can't let you stay much longer," she said.

"I'm going right now. Thanks again, Mrs. Estes."

"Could you do me a favor before you go, Dave?" said Carla. "Close that bathroom door."

Jennifer backed away from the door. She heard Dave grab the handle and then a slight squeak as the door shut all the way. All she could see in the pitch dark was the light from Carla's lamp under the door. After a few moments, it, too, went out.

Jennifer groped in the darkness, found the toilet seat, and sat down. Now she was stuck waiting here until she was sure that Carla was asleep.

PINE

Twelve

Jennifer sat in the bathroom for what felt like an eternity. Finally she heard Carla snoring again. It was the most beautiful sound she had ever heard. When she left the room, she tiptoed down the hall and out the back door of the hospital. The jogging path next to the river was well-lit, and she ran on it until she reached the apartment complex where the school bus had dropped her and Tasha the day before.

She found a pay phone in the all-night Laundromat and called the car service. She didn't feel scared waiting, because there were two Indian women waiting for the dryers to stop. They talked quickly in their native language and glanced at Jennifer nervously a few times.

It was almost 3:30 when Jennifer finally got home. She remembered to deactivate the door alarm this time, and she took her shoes off before climbing the stairs.

She stole a look in her mother's room.

"That you, baby?" her mother called out groggily.

"Yes," said Jennifer as sleepily as she could. Her mother murmured and turned over.

Jennifer pulled the sheets off her bed and took out the bunched-up pillows and the pair of boots she had placed there. She undressed quickly and settled into the cool sheets. Sleep came.

After homeroom Jennifer saw Dave in the hallway talking to Stu Darnell from the basketball team. He broke off the conversation and joined Jennifer as she walked down the hall. He looked tired but happy.

"You're in a good mood," said Jennifer casually.

"Yeah, I guess so." He grinned at her. "Remember that talk we had in your front yard the other day? I got over that. I saw Sarah yesterday."

"That's wonderful," said Jennifer. Her eyes were wide and admiring. "I knew you would, Dave. Sarah's lucky to have a guy like you."

"I just wish I'd done it sooner. She doesn't look as bad as I thought she would." He stopped walking with her. "I'm going the other way," he said, pointing to the opposite end of the hall. "I'll see you later."

As she watched Dave walk away, Jennifer couldn't resist. "I'm proud of you, Dave," she called out after him. "You're a real *mensch*!"

Dave whirled around. Jennifer flashed a sweet, innocent smile.

* * *

"Exhibit A," said Kwame, holding up a cafeteria lunch menu. He lowered his voice and tried to sound like a trial lawyer. "Yesterday they gave us mixed vegetables as a side order. It had carrots, peas, corn, and lima beans. Exhibit B," he said, pointing to a new list. "Today they gave us vegetable soup. It has carrots, peas, corn, and lima beans! Coincidence? I think not."

"So what?" said Cindy. "You don't expect them to throw out the vegetables they had left over, do you? That would be wasteful."

"Yeah, but we pay for fresh food, and they're giving us day-old vegetables. It makes you wonder what else they've been 'recycling' back there. Do they take the old chicken patties and put them in chicken soup? What about the hamburger today?" Kwame pointed to the menu. "Is that tomorrow's Sloppy Joe?"

"I just had a sick thought," said Robert Thornton. "What if they reuse the stuff we leave on the tray! Once it goes in that conveyor belt, we never see it again."

"Robert, do you mind? I'm trying to eat here," cried Tasha. She crunched on a carrot stick. "Did you find out anything more about April and Steve?" she asked Cindy.

Cindy shook her head.

"I tried to talk to Steve about it," Kwame broke in. "You know, man to man. He wouldn't tell me anything. But whatever it is, it's eating him up."

Steve walked past them and set his lunch tray down a few tables away. A dark blue sweater covered the gray turtleneck he had been wearing most of the week. Cindy stood up and went to his table. Tasha followed her.

"Do you mind?" Steve growled. "I'm trying to eat." Kwame and Robert Thornton caught up to the girls as they surrounded Steve. Steve shot hostile glances at all of them.

"Put that food down and talk to us," said Cindy. Steve dropped the orange he was peeling and glared at her. "What's going on with you and April?" she demanded.

"Nothing!" Steve snarled. "Only none of you wants to believe it. What did she say happened?"

"She says you attacked her!" Cindy said.

"What!" Steve said, so loudly that the cafeteria noise died down for a moment. A lunch monitor shot their table a dirty look.

"She didn't say that," Kwame spoke up.

"It's true, Steve, she didn't say that," Tasha chimed in. She saw that Cindy was trying to hush her. "All we know is that April's been acting strange all week, and so have you. Ever since you two were alone Sunday night."

Abruptly Steve stood up. He wrestled his sweater off and threw it on his chair. For a second, his friends thought he was getting ready to fight. Then he hooked the top of the gray turtleneck with his finger and pulled it aside. His friends gasped at the oval bruise, tinged with yellow, that he'd exposed. "Satisfied?" he said.

"A hickey?" said Cindy.

Robert Thornton put his hand over his mouth and stifled a laugh. Steve's face was bright pink as he sat down, picked up the half-peeled orange, and continued tearing off the skin. "Big joke, huh?" Steve snapped. "April gave me a hickey. I told her I didn't like it and she did it anyway. Now will you just leave me alone?"

Nobody moved. Nobody spoke, either. Tasha stole a look at Cindy, who was still frowning at Steve.

"I don't believe April is upset just because you got mad at her for that."

"I don't care what you think, Cindy. Ask her yourself, if you don't believe me."

Cindy pursed her lips in embarrassment. "I was trying to protect April," she muttered.

"Yeah," said Steve with a harsh laugh. "By accusing me of taking advantage of her! I told you it was no big deal, and you didn't believe me. From now on, keep your nosy face out of other people's business!" He tore the orange apart and looked at it a moment. Then he picked up the tray and headed for the trash bucket.

"Look," said Robert Thornton, following him. "It's not that big a deal. It'll go away in a couple more days. Shoot, my brother *collects* them."

"I don't care about your brother, Robert. Not every guy wants to walk around with this thing like it's a major love trophy." He strode back to his table and grabbed his books off it. "Who else thinks I attacked her?" he said to Cindy. "Who do I have to show this to, so they don't think I'm a freak?" He pointed to his neck. "Or will you just start a new rumor?"

He stormed off, with Kwame and Robert following him. Cindy stared after him. When she faced Tasha, her eyes were filled with tears. "I was just trying to protect April," she said.

"You were trying to help," said Tasha. "You did what you thought was right."

Cindy nodded at her gratefully.

"But since it was a mistake," Tasha went on gently, "I think Steve deserves an apology."

"Are you crazy?" Cindy shook her head. "I didn't do anything wrong. Besides, he humiliated me in front of the whole school." She stormed off.

"Steve humiliated *you*?" Tasha called after her.

April approached Tasha a few minutes later. She looked like the queen of the preppies. She had on a wraparound plaid skirt and scuffed brown penny loafers. Her dark red sweater made her blond hair look white.

"Have you seen Cindy?" April asked.

"She's worried about you and Steve," said Tasha. "Whatever got you so mad at Steve, it must have been serious."

April blushed deeply. "Well, it's not that serious. In fact, it's kind of stupid," she said, "that's what's so embarrassing." Tasha kept her face blank as April recounted what Tasha had just heard from Steve.

When Jennifer hurried outside the school building, Kwame was waiting for her on the low stone wall that surrounded the flagpole. He jumped up when he saw

101

her and pulled her toward one of the school buses idling at the curb.

"Remember that white guy I told you about? The one with the broken nose? He's on that bus."

"And you want us to get on the bus with him and follow him to where he lives, is that right?" Kwame nodded. "Forget it, Kwame. We've got nothing on him."

"It's the only lead we have," he said. "Maybe it's not him, but we have to make sure. Otherwise, you look like a liar to the police, to your friends, and everybody else."

Jennifer hesitated. Wouldn't Jim Gardiner know they were following him? she wondered. Before she could make up her mind, the doors on the school bus closed. It started forward with a roar. "It's just as well," said Jennifer.

Kwame looked at her in frustration. Suddenly he ran out to the middle of the road and waved to a car that was pulling out of the student parking lot. Dave slowed and rolled down his window as Kwame talked and gestured. "Come on, Jennifer," Kwame shouted. "Let's go."

Reluctantly Jennifer approached the car. This was a crazy idea, but what did she have to lose?

"Are you sure about this?" Dave said, giving Kwame a doubtful look.

Kwame shrugged. "I think it's worth a try."

The bus had turned north and was heading toward the outskirts of town. But when Dave had to brake for a light, they lost sight of it. They cruised straight ahead and saw two yellow buses.

"Which one do I follow?" asked Dave.

"We were following Bus Twenty. I know a girl who takes that bus to Nutting Road. Let's cut across town and meet them there," said Jennifer.

Dave drove to the Nutting Road Apartments and parked. They waited five minutes. Two buses drove past them before a third finally slowed down and opened its doors.

"Bingo," Kwame said. "There's Bus Twenty."

"That's great," Dave said, "if he's still on it. He could have gotten out already."

"Let's just follow the bus a little longer," Kwame urged.

The bus started and stopped, letting out students in groups of three or four. The longer they followed, the farther away from town they got. Gradually the buildings went from three- and four-story offices to single-story fast-food chains and automobile repair shops. Then they entered a shabby neighborhood with several large bare lots. Frame houses with sagging porches and junk-filled lawns whizzed past.

The bus turned right and traveled on a bumpy road for about half a mile. It drove past a trailer park and then stopped. When the bus opened its doors, three boys and a girl got out. The last boy had a bandage on his nose, and he limped.

Jennifer's heart began to beat faster. "There he is!" she cried.

Dave parked the car abruptly, and the three of them watched the boy limping to his front door. His modest house had white aluminum siding and black shutters. It stood on the edge of the trailer park. Behind the house, a stubbly cornfield stretched toward the interstate. Jennifer's eye was on the two-car garage that stood a few feet away from the house. Both doors were closed and padlocked.

Jennifer got out of the car and headed for the house. Dave and Kwame followed her.

"What are you going to say?" Dave asked.

"I don't know," Jennifer admitted. "But I want to see him close up. I might remember him from the accident." She knocked on the front door and waited. She heard thumping inside, and the door opened.

A short, overweight woman with iron-gray hair and a sour expression looked out. "If this is about charity, we have our own church," she said. She slammed the door, which sent the neighbor's dog into a barking frenzy.

Jennifer rang the doorbell a second time. The woman reappeared.

"Mrs. Gardiner, we're from Jim's school. We wondered if we could talk with him for a few minutes."

"He's taking a nap," she said.

"But we just saw him go inside. Please. It's just for a few minutes."

"I told you, he's taking a nap," Mrs. Gardiner insisted.

"Could we talk with his brother?" said Kwame politely.

Jennifer gave him a quizzical look. Suddenly she remembered the story Jim had told the teacher about his broken nose.

Mrs. Gardiner smirked. "Sure you can talk to his brother," she said. "He's stationed in the Pacific. Hurry or you'll miss him." She closed the door.

Jim *had* lied about the fight! Jennifer thought triumphantly. She knocked one last time. Mrs. Gardiner raised the front window. "Look, you kids," she shouted, "either you get off my property or I call the cops!"

Kwame took Jennifer's arm and pulled her gently toward the car while Dave ran over toward the locked garage.

"Did you see how nervous she was?" Jennifer said to Kwame.

"Yeah," he agreed. "She's hiding something."

"We have to come back," said Jennifer firmly.

"I tried to look inside the windows," Dave said breathlessly when he came back to his car. "But they have boards leaning against them. I checked under the garage door, though. Whatever they drive has big tires."

Kwame unzipped his book bag and took out a folder. "Here, Jennifer, I almost forgot." He took out several photocopied sheets and handed them to her. "Those are hood ornaments and animal logos from all the different kinds of trucks I could find. See if any of them rings a bell."

Jennifer looked at the papers: a bighorn sheep, a

bulldog, a horse rearing up on hind legs, a cartoon coyote. Kwame's face fell as she flipped through them all without stopping. "None of them clicks," she said. "But you're sweet to go to all this trouble. And your hunch about Jim Gardiner was right." She leaned over and gave him a quick kiss on the cheek.

His disappointed look gave way to an awkward grin. He mumbled thanks and reached for his book bag again. Jennifer giggled as several of his books tumbled out on his lap. His advanced algebra book flew open. A previous student had put a bumper sticker across the inside front cover. Jennifer had often observed Kwame scraping pieces of it off with the end of his pen. Now only a few tattered bits of sticker remained: a piece of the big "M" and the small "y" in "Murphy"; and the old version of Wally the mascot, which had recently been replaced by a grinning cartoon. . . .

"That's it!" Jennifer shrieked. She grabbed the math book out of her startled friend's hands. "You found it! You found it!"

Kwame stared at her blankly. Then it clicked. "Jim used to be the equipment manager for the football team. Maybe he has an old Murphy High decal on his truck?"

As Dave started the car, Jennifer was lost in her thoughts. She remembered the slick road and the thick gray sky and then the look on Sarah's face when Jennifer glanced in her direction.

Sarah cringed as she lurched away from her door.

106

The truck that was barreling toward them filled the passenger window. The grille loomed larger and larger. In one of the lower corners of the truck's windshield was a bright decal in the vivid red and gold colors of Murphy High.

Jennifer shuddered as the memory of the impact flooded her brain. Kwame looked at her nervously.

"Jim Gardiner ran into us," said Jennifer quietly. "I'm positive." She told them about the flashback she had just experienced.

Suddenly Dave glanced in the rearview mirror. "Uh-oh," he muttered.

Jennifer and Kwame turned to see a police car pulling up behind them, its lights spinning and flashing.

Thirteen

A policewoman approached their car with her hand resting on the flashlight that hung from her belt. She craned her neck as she looked in the car.

"Everything all right in here?" she said casually. She was a tall black woman with a long face.

"No trouble, Officer," Dave said, trying to sound cheerful. The walkie-talkie in the policewoman's belt squawked. She asked to see Dave's license, registration, and insurance. Dave obediently handed them to her. She walked back to the squad car with them.

Kwame, Dave, and Jennifer looked at each other. "What did I do?" Dave moaned. The woman came back and asked them to step out of the car.

"Can you tell us what this is all about?" said Jennifer.

"Just step out of the car, please," said the woman, giving her a blank look. They got out. Passing motorists slowed down to gape at them as they stood by the highway.

"We got a call about three young black kids harassing a home on Gunderland Road," she said, looking at each one of them. "The car you're driving fits the description. Could you please come to the squad car?"

Dave swore softly as he and the others followed the policewoman. Jennifer saw another policeman get out of the car and walk toward them. She recognized the small build and the dark hair.

"I know you," said Officer Edelman to Jennifer. He gestured to the policewoman that he wanted to talk to Jennifer alone. Jennifer watched as Kwame and Dave were herded into the backseat of the police car. Officer Edelman put his hand on Jennifer's shoulder and led her away from the squad car. "What were you kids doing on Gunderland Road?" he asked.

"If I told you, would you believe me?" Jennifer asked.

Officer Edelman smiled. "Try me."

Jennifer told him about the boy with the broken nose and how they had followed him home. She described the flashback she had when she saw the goat. "If you could take us to the house and open their garage, I bet I can prove the whole thing," she said.

"I guess we could," said Officer Edelman with a sigh. "But we would need a search warrant, and I can't get one based on what you just told me."

"So you're just going to let him get away with it?" Jennifer said.

"I'm going to go talk to Mrs. Gardiner," he said. "If she lets me open the garage, I'll check out your story. If she doesn't, I'll have to go the long legal way, but I'll keep the case open; I promise."

Jennifer gave him a grateful look. "So you're not going to arrest us?"

"No," he said. "But only if you promise not to go back to Mrs. Gardiner's house until I look into things. I don't care if she takes out an ad in the paper that says, 'My son is a hit-and-run driver.' I don't want to see you there."

Jennifer nodded. Officer Edelman walked toward the police car and had a few hushed words with the policewoman. Finally she walked to the backseat and opened it, motioning Dave and Kwame out.

"What did you tell him?" Dave asked Jennifer as they climbed back into the compact Dodge.

"I told him all about Jim Gardiner," she said. "Then I batted my pretty lashes and told him to release the two of you at once, or I would have his badge!"

Fourteen

It was dark when Dave dropped Jennifer off in front of her house. Her mother's car was in the driveway and the light in the living room was on. Her mother was looking out the window as Jennifer got out of the car. "Shoot!" Jennifer said softly. She twisted her key in the front door and pushed it open, bracing herself for the worst.

"Nice of you to make it!" Mrs. Wilson snapped. She was still dressed in her gray suit and pink silk blouse.

"Mom, before you—"

"Before I what, Miss Wilson? When your mother gives you a curfew, you come home straight from school, d'you hear me?"

"But, Mom, it's about the truck I kept—"

"Give it a rest, Jennifer!" her mother snapped. "It's over and done with. Forget about that truck of yours."

She waved the letter in her hand. "This is from Mr. Plint. They're going to raise my insurance premium by twenty percent because of your accident!"

Jennifer lowered her head and fought the urge to cry. She hoped her mother was finished, but Mrs. Wilson was just getting started. "Do I have to take time off from work and come home every day from now on to make sure you're obeying me?" she said. "I work very hard, girl. And I'm doing it alone, without your daddy. I demand your cooperation. If you're not willing to respect me, then there's the door."

"Mom, please listen," Jennifer pleaded. "I was trying to clear my name!"

"You really believe that truck story, don't you?" said Mrs. Wilson, shaking her head in frustration.

"It's the truth. We have proof." Jennifer began to tell her about Jim Gardiner and the rest of the afternoon, but she stopped when she noticed the faraway look in her mother's eyes. She's not paying attention, Jennifer realized.

"You didn't even bother to call," Mrs. Wilson said wearily. "I started to worry about you. Then you drive up in Dave Hunter's car after I explicitly forbid you to ride with your friends."

"I'm sorry, Mom, but—"

"No 'I'm sorry, Mom,' " said Mrs. Wilson. "Hand me your purse." Jennifer gave it to her. Mrs. Wilson took out the wallet and pulled out all of her credit cards. "No more catalog orders," she said firmly. "I returned all the clothes you ordered from my Spangle catalog. If you can't obey a curfew, you aren't responsible enough to have these." She put the cards in her jacket pocket and walked into the kitchen.

"Mom, please! I still have to buy my Christmas gifts. Ground me for another month, but don't take my cards."

"Why should I ground you at all? You won't obey me anyway," said Mrs. Wilson. She sat down at the small kitchen table, her body sagging in the chair.

"Mom, is there anything else wrong?" Jennifer asked. Her mother seemed so defeated.

Mrs. Wilson's expression didn't change. "It's nothing. Go upstairs and do your homework."

"It's Robert, isn't it?"

"Please, baby, just go upstairs."

It *was* about Robert, Jennifer thought, as she went upstairs. The two of them must have had an argument. Jennifer knew that her mother really liked Robert; she wondered what had caused their fight. It's not my fault, she told herself defensively. Why does she have to take it out on me?

As Jennifer threw her book bag on her desk, her eye fell on the photograph of her father. Dr. Wilson's hair had gone prematurely gray, which made him look dignified. In the picture he had his arms around Jennifer, his cheek pressed against hers. "I'll see you after Christmas, when I get back from Europe," his last letter had said. She remembered the huge battle her parents had had over custody of Jennifer. On days like this she wished she were living with her father.

After an hour of trying to do homework, Jennifer

looked at the books she still had to read: history and chemistry. I should've done the chemistry and gotten it out of the way, she told herself. She opened the book to the assigned page. Mr. Hennerly tried hard to make chemistry fun, but no matter what he did, it was still chemistry. "Break time," she said aloud as she stretched out on her bed.

At that moment her mother opened the door. It never fails, Jennifer observed, you work like a maniac for an hour, and they walk in when you're on your butt!

Mrs. Wilson had changed out of her gray suit. She had on a pair of burgundy slacks and a white denim shirt. Her hair was combed back and pinned in place with tortoiseshell barrettes. She looked more like Jennifer's older sister than ever.

"Jennifer, Robert is coming by in a few minutes," said Mrs. Wilson. "We're going to have a long talk, and we need to speak in private."

"Sure, Mom, I'll stay in my room," Jennifer mumbled. She was still mad at her mother for not listening to her.

"I was thinking . . ." Mrs. Wilson began, ". . . maybe I could drop you off at the mall for a few hours. Would that be all right?" She smiled at Jennifer's surprised look. "We're trying to work a few things out, and it might get . . . uh, loud."

"Fine," Jennifer snapped. "When it's convenient for you, I'm allowed out—is that the rule?"

Mrs. Wilson stared at her daughter. "You and I will talk later, young lady."

Jennifer climbed into the car and slumped against the passenger window. They rode in silence past the scene of the accident. The car and the yellow police tape were gone, but the steamroller was still in the exact spot where it had been last Saturday. Jennifer glanced at her mother, but she was preoccupied with her own thoughts.

At the mall Mrs. Wilson handed her daughter some bills. "Here's some money for dinner and a movie. Call me when you're ready to come home."

Jennifer took them without a word and climbed out, slamming the door behind her.

Jennifer walked past the shops she knew so well. She forced herself not to look too long at the window in front of Ms. Tique. The sign announced a new shipment of sweaters from Italy. A saleslady who knew her by name waved as she walked by. One of the stores had an electric-blue prom dress in the window. Jennifer automatically reached for her credit card before she remembered that her mother had taken it.

"Well, look who's here," said a faintly Southern voice. Miss Essie was walking toward her. "How're you?"

Tasha came out of Susan's Nuts! with a small paper bag. "I got the pecans, Miss Essie. Hey, I thought you were grounded!" she said to Jennifer.

"I have the night off." Jennifer smirked. "Robert is coming over."

"Why don't you come home with us?" said Miss Essie. "We're going to make some Pecan Delights."

"Never heard of them," Jennifer said.

"It's a secret recipe. I got it from a lady whose husband ran a theater in St. Louis. We were doing a Christmas show on the Chitlin Circuit, which was what us actors called all the black theaters back then . . . Just listen to me go on!" she said, breaking off. "Do you want to come with us?"

"I should call my mother first."

"Don't be bothering her," said Miss Essie. "I'll call her when we get home."

On the way to the Gordons' house, Miss Essie kept them laughing as she told the story of the Pecan Delights. "You got to know how much rum to put in them. Too much ruins them. Too little, and they ain't hittin' on nuthin', as we used to say."

They rode in silence for a while. "How's Sarah?" Jennifer asked Tasha.

"The same," said Tasha. "I'm very worried about my uncle. He hasn't slept at all this week. He and my aunt are at the hospital every day. When he comes home, he sits in the den and stares out the window. He's thinking of asking the assistant principal to take over next week. He wants to take some sick leave."

"Hey!" Jennifer said. "I didn't tell you what happened today!" She told Tasha how the afternoon with Kwame and Dave had gone. "When we get Jim Gardiner for this, I hope your aunt and uncle sue him for everything he's got."

"What do I care about that?" Tasha snapped. "I just want Sarah back."

"You don't have to yell at me, Tasha. You're not the only one who feels bad about your cousin."

"No more talk about Sarah," said Miss Essie. "Tasha, I'm counting on you to help keep your aunt and uncle's spirits up. That's why we're baking my son's favorite dessert, remember?"

The inside of the Gordon home was bursting with flowers. Cut bouquets and potted plants with cards dangling from them covered every available surface. The dining room still had the remains of dinner on it. Allison, who was supposed to be clearing the dishes, had been taking them into the kitchen one at a time and rewarding herself for each trip by going to the den and watching a bit of her TV program.

"Allison," Miss Essie snapped. "Why aren't these dishes done?"

Allison backed out of the den slowly, her eyes still focused on the TV. "Just a minute, Grandma, this is the really *boocher* part."

"I don't care if it's *boocher, gorly,* or *fa fa foo foo.* You finish putting away those dishes, y'hear?"

Allison pouted as she walked to the dining table. She shot Jennifer a look as if she were to blame.

"I thought she'd be tired of that made-up language by now," said Tasha. She measured the pecans and dropped them into the bowl.

"I think it's cute," said Miss Essie, tying her apron. She pulled the scoop out of the flour bin. "It's a heck of a lot better than walking around the house with a paper crown on your head and calling yourself a princess."

117

"Yeah, but I was eight years old," Tasha protested.

"You made your parents call you 'Your Highness' for a month," said Miss Essie. "Your mother would call me and ask, 'Isn't she too old for this?' " She picked up a small ceramic cup and showed it to the girls as she poured the rum right up to the lip. "The secret is in this cup," she said. "It measures a little more than a measuring cup, but it makes all the difference in the world. That theater lady gave it to me, and someday I'll pass it on to you or Sarah, whoever likes to bake."

Jennifer shuddered. Miss Essie made it sound as though Sarah were just upstairs.

After precisely seventy turns with a wooden spoon, they began to drop thick gobs of batter onto the baking sheet. "What do you want me to set the timer for, Miss Essie?" said Jennifer.

"Never mind that," the old woman said. "Every oven is different. Pecan Delights are ready when you can smell them in the next room."

Tasha and Jennifer cleaned up the kitchen as Miss Essie went to the den to call Mrs. Wilson. Afterward Tasha motioned Jennifer to follow her upstairs. Jennifer noticed that the colorful collage was no longer hanging in the hallway.

Tasha's room was even messier than her own, Jennifer noted with a hint of triumph. Her desk was covered with long strips of colored paper. The news clipping about the accident was glued to a large piece of posterboard. Around it Tasha had stuck a strip of yellow

118

police tape and a photograph of a rain-spattered window.

"That collage is even better than the other one," said Jennifer. She picked up a photograph of Sarah and looked at it.

"I'm still working on it," said Tasha. "It needs something from you." She handed Jennifer a blank sheet of paper and a pen.

"What do you want me to say?" said Jennifer.

"Whatever you feel about what happened," said Tasha.

Jennifer thought for a moment. Then she wrote, "If you can read this, it means you are better. It means you are home. It means you can forgive me and we can be friends again. Love, J." She handed the sheet back to Tasha.

Tasha smiled. "That's beautiful," she said.

Jennifer flushed. She had never gotten a compliment from Tasha before. And never realized how much it would mean to her. "Thanks," she murmured.

Tasha smiled. "Come on. Help me work on this thing."

Jennifer felt happy and hopeful as they worked on the collage together, pasting on pictures of smiling friends and inspirational quotes and song lyrics. The heating vent under Tasha's desk suddenly came to life, and Jennifer savored the cozy warmth.

Suddenly Jennifer could smell the cookies. "The Pecan Delights!" she cried.

Tasha was already out the door. The lightning-quick

legs that intimidated on the basketball court took the stairs two at a time.

"Don't bother running," said Miss Essie. She pointed at the two trays of golden-brown cookies. "I got to them in time. When you can smell them in the next room, I said—not upstairs, down the hall, second door on the left!"

Jennifer and Tasha giggled.

"Wait until they're cool," said Miss Essie, slapping Tasha's hand away. She looked at Jennifer with mock pain. "I tried to raise her right."

The phone rang and Tasha went to pick it up, but Allison announced that she had it.

"Don't give me that sad puppy look," said Miss Essie to Tasha. "Go ahead and take some." They each took two.

"They're totally sinful," said Jennifer through the crumbs.

Allison came in and took a cookie in each hand. "Cindy is on the *bring*," she said. "I told her Jennifer was here, and she said to put you both on."

"You stay here," Tasha told Jennifer. "I'll pick up in the den."

"Hey, Cindy, what's up?" Jennifer said. She heard a click as Tasha joined them on the line.

"Did you hear the rumor Steve has been spreading about *me*?"

"What!"

"Do you know Amanda Dennis?" Cindy began. "She's that girl on the gymnastics team who hangs out with Debby Barnes and her crowd. Today I'm in the bathroom and she asks me if it's true I slept with Dave DiPetta!"

"That's just stupid," said Jennifer. "Everyone knows you're not interested in him." Dave DiPetta was a white boy who had recently shaved his head and had his nose pierced.

"Amanda is just goofing on you," Tasha assured her. Amanda was part of Debby Barnes's group of stuck-up friends, all of whom liked to gossip. Everyone knew that Debby, who was leader of the Pep Squad, loved to cause trouble.

"That's what I thought," said Cindy. "Until I went to choir class. Who's waiting at the door but Dave DiPetta. He tells me in front of everybody to quit telling people we had done it. I was so mad at him, I almost kicked him."

"You should have," Tasha and Jennifer chorused.

"Do you think Steve started the rumor?" Tasha asked.

"Of course! It's his stupid way of getting me back for what happened with April. I'm going to get him for this," Cindy said icily.

"Look, you'd better make sure he's behind this," Jennifer said.

"Whose side are you on, Jennifer Wilson? He's trying to teach me a lesson. Give me a taste of my own medicine. Well, that boy picked the wrong person to mess with."

"What are you going to do?" said Tasha.

"If he wants rumors, I'll give him rumors," said Cindy vehemently. "I'll make it so he can't show his face in school."

"Look, Cindy. Why don't you just call Steve and talk it out," said Tasha. "The two of you are acting like kids."

"Easy for you to say, Tasha," Cindy snapped. "It isn't happening to you."

That was the wrong thing to say, Jennifer thought. She winced when Tasha's voice burst through the receiver.

"That's right!" Tasha shot back. "It isn't happening to me. My cousin is in the hospital in a coma and you want me to care about an argument between two of my friends who are acting like babies! Well, I don't have any sympathy to spare, Cindy Phillips. If you had apologized to Steve during lunch, it wouldn't have gone this far."

Jennifer heard a loud click as Tasha slammed down the phone. "Cindy," she said, "just call Steve and talk it out, okay?"

"I will never speak to Steve Adams or Tasha Gordon as long as I live!" Cindy cried. She slammed her phone down. Jennifer stood frozen in place, the phone pressed against her ear, until the dial tone buzzed again.

Allison walked into the kitchen and took three more Pecan Delights. "These cookies are *tula boocher*," she said. "Tasha's in a *gorly* mood. What happened?"

Tasha suddenly opened the kitchen door and looked

122

at her young cousin. "I can't believe Cindy Phillips sometimes!" she said. "Allison, did you and Pam come up with a word for 'stubborn as a mule'?"

Allison gave her an anguished look. "Yes, but I don't think you're going to like it."

"It better not be *tasha*," Tasha warned.

Allison just smiled.

Fifteen

A light rain hit the windshield as Miss Essie drove Jennifer home. A bag of Pecan Delights sat between them on the front seat.

Most of Jennifer's anger at her mother had disappeared and she found herself hoping that her mother had patched things up with Robert. She tried to imagine calling him Dad, but she couldn't hear herself saying it. Not yet. She liked having her mother all to herself and she wasn't completely ready to give up the hope of her parents getting back together. I guess I can get used to Robert, she thought, if he makes Mom happy. And maybe things between Jennifer and Robert would start to change for the better. They already had between her and Tasha. Two weeks ago Jennifer would have laughed if anybody had told her they would spend an evening alone together. "I guess anything is possible," she murmured.

Miss Essie heard her and sighed. "It is at sixteen!"

That night, as Jennifer lay in bed, she felt more relaxed than she had in days. Her mother had looked happy when Jennifer came in from the Gordons'. Robert had just left.

"I'm too tired to go into detail," Mrs. Wilson had said to Jennifer's persistent questions. "But I promise you'll get a full report." Mrs. Wilson picked up the cocktail glasses from the coffee table and hummed a Motown tune. It was one of the nicest sounds Jennifer had heard in a while.

But things turned sour almost as soon as Jennifer woke up the next day. First she couldn't find the gold necklace she wanted to wear over her violet turtleneck. The cream-colored slacks she put on turned out to be much too thin for the raw weather, and she shivered all the way to school. As if that wasn't enough, one of the yearbook photographers snapped a picture of her just as she was touching up her makeup by her locker.

"Don't you dare print that picture in the yearbook," she warned the shy senior boy. She hoped she had scared him enough.

In chemistry class Jennifer watched the clock, willing it to move faster.

"What is Pb the chemical symbol for? Jennifer?"

Jennifer looked at Mr. Hennerly blankly, hoping he would go to another student. But he waited.

"Platinum?" replied Jennifer weakly.

"Don't buy Pb thinking it's platinum," said Mr.

Hennerly with a grin. "You'll be spending a fortune on lead."

The class giggled as Jennifer looked down at her desk. "Good going," she mumbled to herself.

After class Mr. Hennerly called her to his desk for one of his famous "discussions." She had to wait several minutes while he spoke to someone else from her class. When it was her turn, he smiled gently at her.

"You got it right on the homework, but you missed it in class," he said. "I know you have a lot on your mind and I'm concerned about you. Is everything okay?"

Jennifer nodded. "I'll be fine." The bell for the next period rang, and she asked Mr. Hennerly for a hall pass. He gave it to her.

She took her time going to French class. The substitute teacher had promised to show a movie today, and it would probably be as silly and boring as the other ones she'd seen. She turned the corner of the hallway and almost collided with a tall white boy. She looked at his right knee, which was wrapped in a thick cloth, and then saw the bandage that covered the bridge of his nose.

"You're Jim Gardiner!" she exclaimed.

Jim looked at her for a moment and began to limp away.

"You ran into me near Dawes Highway last Saturday, didn't you?" said Jennifer, catching up to him.

"I don't know what you're talking about," he growled.

"Why didn't your mom let us talk to you yesterday?"

"Because I got nothing to say to you."

"How did you break your nose?"

"I had a fight with my brother," he said over his shoulder.

"Your brother is in the Pacific."

At that Jim turned around and gave her a fiery look.

"You have to tell the police what really happened," said Jennifer. "My friend is in the hospital because of what you did."

"I can't bring Sarah Gordon back," he cried. There was fear in his blue eyes. "I'm not going to lose my license for no reason."

"Then you admit you ran me off the road?" Jennifer asked.

"It's your word against mine," he said, looking down at his shoes.

Jennifer wished there were someone to overhear this conversation. "So you're going to let me take the blame for the accident?"

"I'm sorry," he said.

"'I'm sorry' doesn't cut it," retorted Jennifer angrily. "I'm going to find a way to prove you were involved if it's the last thing I do."

"And I'll deny everything you say," he snapped. He looked at her pleadingly. "If I turn myself in, I'll lose my license. I've already got an accident on my record. If they nail me, I won't be able to drive for three years. Three years! You don't think I feel bad about what happened, but I do. I just can't let them take away my license."

Jennifer looked at him coldly. "Do what you think you have to do, Jim," she said. "I'll do what I have to do."

They stared at each other for a minute; then Jim turned and limped away. Jennifer walked quickly to French class.

Jennifer was one of the first students to leave the building that day. Without bothering to get her coat, she ran to the student parking lot and checked out all the pickup trucks there. None of them looked badly dented or had the old-fashioned mascot sticker. She stopped looking when she spotted Jim Gardiner limping toward a bus. Fool, she said to herself. Why would he drive the truck to school? He was on the bus yesterday.

"Jennifer, you're going to get pneumonia!" April cried as Jennifer returned to the building.

April was holding Steve's hand and wearing one of his sweaters again, Jennifer observed. When she told them about the conversation with Jim Gardiner, April's eyes flashed.

"What a sleaze!" she said.

Steve nodded grimly.

"Hey," said Kwame as he approached. "The three of you look like you're plotting to overthrow the principal. In case you forgot, it's Friday!" When they told him about Jennifer's hallway encounter, he let out a low whistle. "We'll get him," Kwame said confidently.

"Steve and I are going to 18 Pine St.," said April. "Afterwards we're going to stop by the hospital."

Kwame agreed to join them.

"I can't. I have to go home," said Jennifer. She sprinted to her locker, picked up her coat, and barely made her bus.

She stared out the dusty windows at the dead grass on the lawns and the black trees. November was a terrible weather month, she decided. No pretty leaves, and not enough snow.

The bus let her off, and Jennifer ran quickly down her street. She was glad when she spotted her mother's car in the driveway. Let her see me coming home on time, she thought.

Jennifer made a big show about walking into the house. She gave her mother a sweet, obedient, responsible hug, then dropped her book bag and went to the refrigerator for a diet soda.

"Keep your jacket on," said Mrs. Wilson, tying her Burberry scarf around her head. "We're going to the hospital. I haven't talked to the Gordons in days." Her eyes moistened and she dabbed at them with a tissue. "You kids grow up too fast. I ought to lock you in the house until you're twenty-five."

"Mom, nothing's going to happen to me," said Jennifer. "Besides, what happened to Sarah was an accident, remember?"

"I know, but you'll understand how I feel when you're a mother—"

"—'and you have a sixteen-year-old daughter,' " Jennifer finished for her.

On the way to the hospital Mrs. Wilson began telling

her about her discussion with Robert. "We had a big argument over the phone yesterday and I needed to straighten out a few things with him." She cast a sidelong glance at her daughter.

"Jennifer, how would you feel about having Robert as a stepfather?" she asked cautiously.

Jennifer swallowed hard. "You met him less than two months ago, Mom."

"That doesn't answer my question."

"I'd be happy if you were happy," said Jennifer. She looked out the window so that her mother couldn't read her face.

"You know how I feel about Robert," said Mrs. Wilson. "Last night we talked about getting engaged. But I don't want to rush into anything. My experience with your father has made me very cautious. I want to make sure I'm doing this because I *want* Robert in my life, not just because I get lonely sometimes."

Her mother's last words surprised Jennifer. She'd never really thought about her mother's being lonely. Mrs. Wilson had so much going on all the time. . . .

As she turned toward her mother, Mrs. Wilson reached over and squeezed Jennifer's hand. "This is only the beginning of the discussion, honey; in the meantime you and Robert don't know each other very well. I think the three of us should do something together this weekend. This accident has made me realize that I leave you out of a lot of parts of my life. And I'm sorry about asking you to go to the mall last night. It's your house, too.

Jennifer couldn't speak. She felt too full of too many things—especially love for her mother. She squeezed her mother's hand and said, "Does this mean I get my credit cards back?"

Her mother laughed loudly. "Jennifer Wilson, you're your mother's daughter—that's for sure!"

At the hospital they were given permission to go to Sarah's room. Carla had a Walkman on and she was bopping to the music. She waved to Jennifer and Mrs. Wilson.

Jennifer walked to the partition and opened it. Two chairs were positioned next to Sarah's bed. She imagined Mr. and Mrs. Gordon spending long afternoons keeping vigil next to their silent daughter.

Sarah looked different. Her hair had been worked into many tight braids and fastened in place with gold-tipped hairpins. The scrapes on her face were beginning to heal.

Jennifer watched her mother touch Sarah's hand. Her own thoughts drifted to Jim Gardiner. If she could find a way to get him to see Sarah, he might break down and confess.

They sat quietly for a few minutes longer. Sarah's legs twitched involuntarily a few times and her mouth seemed to be forming words, though no sounds came out.

Mrs. Wilson stood up suddenly. "I'll be right back," she told her daughter. "I promised to call Robert this afternoon. If Mrs. Gordon comes, tell her I'm here with you."

After she left Jennifer looked at Sarah. "We're alone again," she whispered to her friends. Outside a light snow began to fall. Jennifer watched it for a while. Then she noticed that some of Sarah's get-well cards had been knocked over by the air from the heating vents. She got up to straighten the cards. A tall card was wedged in the grating, and Jennifer pulled it out and opened it slightly. She did the same with another one that showed an elf sitting on a big toadstool.

"The sooner you get better . . ." the outside of the card said. "The sooner *I'll* get better!" said the inside. It was signed by Lisa Penia, a girl Jennifer wasn't sure she knew.

"Jennifer."

Jennifer whirled around. She looked at Carla, whose head was still bobbing up and down as she wrote in her notebook.

Then Jennifer noticed Sarah's open eyes.

Sixteen

Jennifer could feel the tears pouring down her cheeks. "We had an accident, Sarah. You're going to be all right."

Sarah closed her eyes, and Jennifer thought she might be slipping away again. Desperately, she looked around for the button that summoned the nurse. "Carla! Carla!" she shouted.

Carla pulled her earphones off. Jennifer found the button and pushed it down, keeping her finger on it. "She talked to me!" Jennifer cried. "We've got to get a nurse."

"I'll help you," Carla shouted. She pressed the emergency button on her own bed. It didn't take long before a nurse and a doctor appeared in the room.

Jennifer looked down and noticed that Sarah's eyes were open again. "Over here," she said to the doctor. She was an Asian woman about Jennifer's height.

"How do you feel, Sleeping Beauty?" said the doctor.

"I'm hungry," mumbled Sarah.

"I'll bet you are." The doctor laughed and beamed a penlight in Sarah's eyes. She looked at the machines that monitored her heartbeat and brain waves. "Welcome back," she said. She asked Jennifer to tell them exactly what had happened when Sarah had regained consciousness. The nurse wrote it down on the clipboard at the end of Sarah's bed.

The door opened, and Mr. and Mrs. Gordon came in with Mrs. Wilson. When Mrs. Gordon saw the nurse and doctor standing next to her daughter, she ran toward her, with Mr. Gordon close at her heels. Her cry of panic turned into a shriek of joy when Sarah turned her head toward her.

Jennifer saw her mother motioning her away from the bed. "Best to leave them alone a little while." She steered her daughter to the hall.

Kwame, April, and Steve were standing around the nurses' station.

"Sarah is awake," Jennifer cried. Her friends shouted and ran toward Sarah's room.

"You kids will have to leave," said the nurse.

"But we came to see Sarah," Steve protested.

"It's too much noise. She's in a delicate situation. She just got out of a coma," said the nurse, motioning them back.

"Are you saying we can't see her because she's *better*?" said Kwame incredulously.

"She's with her mother and father right now," said the nurse. "You can see her tomorrow."

"It's a miracle," said April.

"I'm going to call Tasha," said Kwame, running to a bank of phones down the hall.

"Call Cindy, too," April shouted.

"And Dave!" said Steve.

"Hey," Kwame said, frowning. "I've only got one quarter."

Jennifer giggled. Then her legs got very wobbly and the edges of her vision suddenly went black.

Mrs. Wilson caught her.

Jennifer woke up on a cot in a room behind the nurses' station. Her mother helped her to sit up and then held out a cup of water. Jennifer drank slowly.

"Are you okay, honey?" Mrs. Wilson asked. "You passed out and scared all of us."

"I'm fine," Jennifer said. "I just feel weak."

Mrs. Gordon appeared at the doorway. "How's Jennifer?" she asked Mrs. Wilson.

"Can I go see Sarah now? Please, Mrs. Gordon?"

Sarah's mother hesitated. "Are you up to it?"

"Yes," Jennifer replied eagerly.

"Five minutes," the doctor warned when they rushed in. The doctor had sent the nurse out for some broth and juice from the cafeteria and cranked Sarah into an upright position so that she could drink it.

Sarah smiled at the gang. Mr. Gordon moved aside as they crowded around the bed, but he didn't let go of his daughter's hand.

"I just found out I've been out for a week," said Sarah weakly. "Did anybody get my homework?"

They all laughed. "Don't worry about that," said Jennifer.

"What happened to Jim?" said Sarah.

"There she goes again," Mr. Gordon said softly. "Who is Jim, honey?"

"Jim," Sarah insisted.

It took Jennifer only a second. "You mean Jim Gardiner?"

Sarah nodded. A chill crawled up Jennifer's back.

"I was his math tutor last year," explained Sarah. "Is he all right? That's the last thing I remember seeing— his face behind the steering wheel. I thought he was asleep, or something."

"He's fine," said Jennifer. Actually he's history, she thought. Kwame wore a look of triumph.

"That whole story about the truck is true?" asked Mrs. Wilson. She squeezed Jennifer's shoulder. "Baby, I'm sorry."

"I'm afraid you'll have to go," the doctor said. "Sarah needs to rest."

Sarah gave the doctor a thin smile. "But I just got up!"

Seventeen

The next morning Jennifer's mother called Jim Gardiner's house. Mrs. Gardiner picked up the phone, but she slammed it down when Mrs. Wilson identified herself and brought up the accident. Mrs. Wilson then called the Gordons to decide what to do. Twenty minutes later Jennifer found herself in the front seat of her mother's car, directing her to the Gardiners' house. Tasha and Mr. and Mrs. Gordon were in the car behind.

The grown-ups waited by the Gardiners' front door for someone to appear while Tasha and Jennifer sat in the car.

A police cruiser pulled up to the house. A second squad car arrived from the other end of the street. Mrs. Gordon approached the first squad car by herself and talked to Officer Edelman. She showed him a sheet of paper. Edelman nodded and picked up his two-way radio. A moment later the second squad car pulled away. Jennifer held her breath as Officer Edelman and the tall black policewoman both got out of the car and sauntered up the driveway toward the rest of the adults.

Everyone was surprised to see the automatic garage door tilting open.

Jim Gardiner noticed the parked police cruiser as soon as he turned onto Gunderman Road. He swallowed hard and fought the urge to turn around and drive off. His mother was alone in the house—he had to go home. He forced himself to turn his pickup into the driveway, and pushed the button on the remote control for the garage door.

As the truck passed by, Jennifer saw the iron bars that had been welded across the front end. That's why he didn't break his headlights, she thought. Someone had tried unsuccessfully to hammer a corner of the bumper back into its original shape, but it still looked like crumpled aluminum foil. She pointed out the red and gold sticker on the windshield to Tasha.

Mrs. Gardiner stuck her head out of one of the windows. "Get in the house, Jimmy! Don't talk to anybody, just get in," she shouted.

Jim just sat in the driver's seat, staring sullenly at the people on his doorstep. Mrs. Gardiner disappeared from the window and came out the front door. She pushed past Jennifer and Tasha's parents in a brown bathrobe and floppy brown slippers shaped like puppies. "Leave my son alone!" she shrieked. "Jimmy, get away from here!"

The policewoman motioned Jim out of the truck, and he got out.

"Don't say a word to anybody, Jim," his mother warned.

"Mrs. Gardiner, the boy needs to answer some questions about the accident last Saturday," said Mr. Gordon.

"I ain't talking to anybody without a lawyer," the mother replied.

"Then I suggest you get one," said Mrs. Gordon testily.

"Ma, let me talk to them," Jim said, pulling out of his mother's grip. His eyes went from Mrs. Gordon to Mrs. Wilson, trying to assess who was who. "I'm sorry about Sarah," he mumbled. "I didn't mean to do it."

"It's about time," Tasha murmured. Jennifer nodded.

"Do you admit you were driving that truck down Dawes Highway last Saturday, and that you collided with a . . ." Officer Edelman looked down at the paper Mrs. Gordon had handed to him. ". . . Saab?"

Jim nodded and Mrs. Gardiner started to cry. Jim moved to comfort her. "Don't touch me!" she snapped.

"Ma, I had to tell them," Jim cried, his voice cracking. "It was just going to get worse."

"They're going to take away your license, you idiot! They're going to put you in jail for hit and run and maybe even driving while intoxicated!"

"Let's discuss this from start to finish," said Mr. Gordon. "May we come in, Mrs. Gardiner?"

Defeated, Mrs. Gardiner turned and went back inside, leaving the door open for the others to follow. In the car Tasha and Jennifer traded high fives.

PINE

Eighteen

On Monday morning, a week later, Jennifer was at her locker. She felt great. She had on her black stirrup pants and a bulky gold sweater. She dabbed a little more lip gloss on her mouth and turned her head from side to side in front of the long locker mirror. "Perfect," she told her reflection.

She waited until Kwame walked away from his locker before slipping a bumper sticker, one with the new Wally the Goat mascot, through the vent. On the bottom she had written, "Thanks, Sherlock Holmes. XOXOXO."

During homeroom Assistant Principal Schlesinger read the announcements in his usual monotone. "Finally, I'm pleased to announce that Sarah Gordon is making a speedy recovery from her accident and will rejoin the Murphy High School community soon."

At lunch later that day Jennifer sat down next to

Tasha. "I don't know why, but everybody keeps asking me how Sarah is doing. They should be asking you."

"Tell them she's doing fine," said Tasha. She had braided her beautiful hair and threaded long wooden beads near the ends. "She got home yesterday. She's thin as a rail. And," she said, giving Jennifer an affectionate squeeze on her thigh, "she loved what you put on the collage."

Kwame sat down and put his book bag on the pile in the middle of the table. Jennifer noticed that he had stuck the bumper sticker on the outside of it. "How's Sarah?" he asked them.

"Maybe I should write a bulletin and pass it around," said Tasha. "She's fine, Kwame. She's eating like a horse."

"A good sign," said Kwame, taking a foot-long sandwich out of his book bag.

Next José sat down. "How's Sarah?" he asked. He looked at Tasha and Jennifer curiously when they burst into laughter.

Kwame nudged Jennifer and pointed to the paintings on the wall. "Guess which one won the contest?" Jennifer saw that the scene of the hunters stalking a buck had a round metallic blue sticker stuck on its frame. But she was more interested in the table closest to that wall. Cindy Phillips sat alone, eating an apple and reading a book.

Kwame followed her gaze. "She still mad at Steve?"

"Yeah," Tasha broke in. "She's mad at me, too. I think she kept calling our house last night. Someone kept hanging up on me. Cindy probably wanted to talk to Sarah."

"Someone ought to go and talk to her," Kwame suggested.

When Steve and April sat down, Kwame repeated his suggestion. "Forget it," Steve said sullenly. "Cindy 'accidentally' bumped into me on the stairs outside the computer room. My notebook flew open and now my homework assignment has a big ugly shoe mark on it."

"Fine!" said Jennifer sarcastically. "You two keep acting like babies, see if we care."

"Baby wants your pudding if you're not going to eat it," said Steve, taking the dish from Jennifer's tray.

Robert's car was parked in the driveway when Jennifer got home. She was surprised to see her mother dressed in jeans and a light blue shirt. Didn't she go to work today? Jennifer wondered.

Robert smiled when Jennifer came into the kitchen. He was dressed as casually as her mother: rust-colored corduroy slacks and a blue denim shirt. He's very good-looking, Jennifer admitted. "What's up?" he said.

Jennifer smiled back and looked at her mother meaningfully. "Did you take the day off, Mom?"

"Sort of," Mrs. Wilson said brightly. "The office above mine flooded and it seeped straight through the ceiling."

She's in love, Jennifer realized. Usually when something like that happened, her mother had a fit.

"We've been sitting here talking away the afternoon

and waiting for you to come home," said Mrs. Wilson.

"I wanted to ask you if you wanted to join your mother and me for dinner tonight," said Robert.

"Well, I have a lot of . . ." Homework, Jennifer was about to say. She saw her mother looking at her eagerly. "I'd love to go," said Jennifer quickly.

"Great, I'll make the reservations. Flagstone Inn all right with you?" asked Robert. Jennifer assured him it was, and her mother beamed.

Jennifer ran upstairs to call Tasha. Her friend answered on the first ring.

"Cindy, I know it's you, don't hang up!" Tasha cried.

"It's me, Jennifer."

Tasha sighed. "She just called again a minute ago."

"This has to stop," said Jennifer emphatically. "Steve and April made up; why can't Cindy and Steve do it?"

"Because she won't talk to him, and she won't talk to me," said Tasha, "and she won't listen to anybody else."

"She'll listen to Sarah," said Jennifer. Suddenly an idea began forming in her mind. "Tasha, your uncle has a tool kit, doesn't he?"

The dinner at the Flagstone Inn was more fun than Jennifer thought it would be. Jennifer tried to be charming, laughing at Robert's jokes and answering his questions about Murphy with enthusiasm. It didn't feel forced the way it usually did. Jennifer realized she was warming up to Robert.

After Robert had gone home, Jennifer decided to take advantage of her mother's good mood.

"Mom, since it turned out I was telling the truth about the accident, do you think it's fair to keep me grounded *and* without my credit cards?"

"For the record I punished you because you took the car without my permission, and because you broke the curfew and rode in Dave Hunter's car. I didn't punish you for having an accident," said Mrs. Wilson. "But Robert thinks I should give you a break about the credit cards."

I love him, Jennifer thought. "When?" she cried.

"Soon," said Mrs. Wilson. "End of discussion."

The next day Jennifer made sure she bumped into Cindy after homeroom.

"I have a message from Sarah, Cindy. Tasha tried to tell you, but you won't listen to her. Sarah wants you to come to her house after school."

"Why didn't Sarah call me herself?" said Cindy suspiciously.

"She's still in bed," said Jennifer, feigning impatience. "Besides, she asked Tasha about it this morning."

Cindy slammed her locker shut. "Tell Tasha to tell Sarah I'll be there."

Jennifer caught up with Steve after the next class.

"Sarah wants to see me?" he said.

"She's way, way behind in computer class, and she

144

wants the expert to tutor her," said Jennifer. The word "expert" had the desired effect. Steve puffed up slightly and smiled.

"I'll be there," he assured her.

Everything was going according to plan, Jennifer thought. She hated having to go straight home. She wanted desperately to head to the Gordons' to watch the fireworks she and Tasha were about to create. But she didn't want to risk upsetting her mother. Things were finally going well.

Nineteen

Cindy took the bus home with Tasha, but she sat right behind the driver, while Tasha chatted with her friends in the back. They both got out and walked to the Gordons' house, ignoring each other all the way. Tasha finally broke the silence when Cindy started up the stairs to Sarah's room.

"Wait down here," Tasha ordered. "I'll see if Sarah is awake."

Cindy sighed and paced impatiently by the front door. She tried to concentrate on the multicolored letters Allison had cut out of construction paper that spelled out "Welcome Back, Sarah." After what seemed like an eternity, Tasha finally returned and motioned her upstairs.

While Cindy greeted Sarah with a hug, Steve parked his battered Toyota on the street and bounded up to the Gordons' door. Allison, who had promised not to give

146

away the plan if she could play a role in it, answered the doorbell.

"Stay here, I'll be back *atta dip*," Allison said to a confused Steve. "I just have to see if Sarah's awake."

Tasha signaled to Allison that Cindy was safely inside Sarah's room.

Allison went downstairs and summoned Steve. "Try to be quiet," she warned him. "Sarah is still a little *chickery*."

Steve tiptoed down the hall to Sarah's room and heard low voices. He stood at the doorway for a fraction of a second, which was just long enough for Tasha to run out of the bathroom and give him a firm shove into the room before she shut the door.

"Hey!" Steve cried, catching himself before he fell. He saw Cindy glaring at him.

"Leave us alone, Steve," Cindy shouted.

"Gladly!" he said, shooting an apologetic look to Sarah. He whirled around, grabbed the door handle, and pulled hard. The knob came off in his hand and the door remained closed. He looked at it in bewilderment. Cindy's mouth dropped open as well.

"What is this?" said Steve, looking at Sarah.

"It's called 'forced communication,' " said Sarah sternly. She took a napkin off the tray of Pecan Delights by her nightstand and offered them some. "Get comfortable," she commanded. "Tasha won't put the door back together until I give her the signal. And I won't give her the signal until the two of you are friends again."

"Good luck!" said Cindy. "I'm not talking to that idiot again after what he said about Dave DiPetta and me."

"Is that another one of your stupid rumors, Cindy? What did I say about you and DiPetta? Or do you change it each time?"

"Don't play dumb, Steve!" Cindy shot back.

Sarah calmly ate a Pecan Delight and listened to them shouting at each other. Although their yelling was loud, the sound of her friends resolving their problems was music to Sarah's ears.

Finally, Steve's insistence that he hadn't started the rumor about Dave DiPetta sank in with Cindy. "Okay," she said, "if you didn't start the rumor—and I'm not totally convinced you didn't—then I apologize."

"I didn't, so apology accepted," said Steve. There was a long silence. "You know," he said finally, "as furious as I was with you about what you thought I did, I . . . it was good to see that April has a friend who cares so much about her."

"We all do," said Cindy.

"Me too," said Steve, turning slightly pink.

"Well, that wasn't so bad, was it?" said Sarah. She called out to Tasha, who put the other end of the door-knob back in its place.

But neither Steve nor Cindy made a move for the door. There were still too many cookies left on the tray.

"Well, look who's back!" said Mr. Harris. He smiled at Sarah, who smiled back. She still looked thin, but there was color in her cheeks. "This calls for a celebration," the owner of 18 Pine St. said. He disappeared behind the counter and expertly tossed a lump of dough in the air. José and Kwame rubbed their hands in anticipation.

Dave came up to their table and put a chair next to Sarah. He sat down and gave her a kiss on the lips. Sarah took his hand. She'd never forget what Carla had told her about Dave's midnight visit. "Did you really try to kiss me awake?" she whispered in his ear now.

"I deny everything!" Dave whispered back, but the look on his face had said it all.

Tasha looked at her cousin. "Are you tired, cuz?" she asked.

Sarah grinned. "For the tenth time: No, I'm not tired."

"I was just trying to be nice," Tasha grumbled.

"Don't be nice," said Sarah mischievously. "Just be yourself!" They all laughed.

The Gordon cousins are back to normal, Jennifer thought with relief. I'm glad Mom let me out for Sarah's first day back at school.

"What I still don't get," said Cindy to Steve a minute later, "is the rumor about Dave DiPetta. If you didn't start it, who did?"

"I can answer that," said April. "I overheard Amanda Dennis talking to Debby Barnes in the bathroom near the art courtyard. Debby Barnes said, 'Does she still think it's Steve?' and Amanda said, 'I think so.'"

"Of course!" Cindy cried. "I should have suspected

Debby right off." Debby Barnes was the leader of the pep squad, and, according to a vote once taken in the back of 18 Pine St., she was the most stuck-up girl in the whole school.

"Clear a space," Mr. Harris ordered. Kwame and José took their basket of fries off the table, while Jennifer, Sarah, and Tasha lifted their soda cups. April and Steve leaned back out of the way as Mr. Harris lowered the mammoth pizza onto the table and stepped back to admire his handiwork.

They could barely see any cheese or tomato sauce. Mr. Harris had covered the pie with hamburger, sausage, pepperoni, and anchovies. Tasha, who was trying to be a vegetarian, grimaced.

"It smells amazing," said Kwame dreamily.

"What did you end up calling it?" José asked. "The Round-Up? *El Magnifico*?"

"The Bowser," said Mr. Harris, beaming.

"The Bowser?" echoed José. He tried to sound polite.

"After my first dog," said Mr. Harris. "Loved him like a son. Bowser would do anything for an anchovy," he said wistfully.

"I don't care what it's called," said Kwame through his mouthful, "it's a hit!"

The rest of them, except for Tasha, dug in.

"Hey, Sarah, take it easy!" Kwame said a while later.

They all looked at her plate, where two pizza crusts lay. Sarah was almost finished with her third slice.

Kwame looked with wounded pride at his own plate, which still held more than half of his second slice.

"We have a new pizza king," Steve declared, placing an imaginary crown over Sarah's head. "Sorry, Kwame, you've been usurped."

"Speech! Speech!" José yelled.

Sarah held up her hand and finished swallowing. Then she pointed at Kwame's plate and gave him a friendly smile. "Are you going to finish that, Kwame?"

Jennifer laughed along with the rest of her friends. Sarah was back, and it felt great.

Coming in Book 8,
Dangerous Games

Debby noticed that April, Tasha and Jennifer were paying attention. She explained the rules of the new game, pausing now and then to wait for a passing boy to move out of earshot. "Each girl names a boyfriend," she said. "The way you eliminate a player from the game is by kissing her boyfriend. The winner is the girl whose boyfriend holds out the longest."

Sarah knew that this could be trouble. She also knew that it would be fun. "I'm in," she said with a smile.

When the guys at 18 Pine start playing an assassination game called KAOS, they almost get suspended from school. Sarah and Tasha get angry, but when Debby Barnes suggests they play their own killing game, they don't realize what they're in for.